THE SCORPION'S CLAW

ACKNOWLEDGEMENTS

Sincere thanks go to the readers of earlier draft's of the novel's manuscript, especially to Maritza Stanchich and Sheryl Byfield. Thanks also to the editors of the following publications in which excerpts of the novel previously appeared: NYU's *Black/Renaissance Noire* (1997), *The Louisville Review* (1995) and Toronto's *Fireweed* (1994). Finally, I wish to thank Peepal Tree Press for taking this novel under their wings.

THE SCORPION'S CLAW

MYRIAM J A CHANCY

PEEPAL TREE

First published in Great Britain in 2005
Peepal Tree Press
17 King's Avenue
Leeds LS6 1QS
England

ISBN 1 900715 91 0

Peepal Tree gratefully acknowledges Arts Council support

For
Alice Limousin Chancy
(1920-1995)
and for my mother
Marie-Carmel Adeline Lamour Chancy

CARMEL
1917-1991

"and for those who sat in the region and shadow of death
light has dawned..."
Matthew 4:16

There was a time beyond memory when the morning broke quietly above our heads and the sun grew out of the mountains like a miraculous tree anointing us with fruits ripe with promise.

When the morning broke in this way, there were no crows crying out in the darkness. There were no unshod feet walking through the desolate, half-paved streets leading from the cities to the hidden springs of water in the perilous mountains. There were no wandering spirits looking for a final time of rest. There was only the stillness of a place that had the shape of beauty itself, asking only to be preserved like the rare pearl it was, cradled in the aquamarine blue waters of the ocean which lay playful as a child against soft sandy beaches.

In the time beyond memory, there was no need to wonder how food would find its way onto tables, clothing upon the backs of the children crouching by the rivers, watching their mothers clean tripe in the fresh, running water. Beyond memory there is only that place where we yearn to return, but which can only evade us since it has never truly been. In that place there are dreams laying themselves open like the pages of picture books. It is a place where we can take nothing but our souls and the memories of our elders who carved out the paths to freedom, only to see us walk away from their bosoms, clutching anger like thunderbolts in our tight fists. We did not realize that we would be called back to the place we despised, crooned to unfurl our fingers and embrace the home we had tried in vain to remove from our memories.

It was on the day I dreamed of the father of my children that I began to see the world more fully, as if I had eyes in the back of my head, on my shoulders, and on the tips of my fingers. I had lived for over sixty years in this small house, three rooms large, with an oven at the back I treasured more than any jewel. I could remember well my mother opening the wooden door to slide in the mounds of dough which would turn into rich brown bread. We ate it with home-made peach preserves sent up from the *faubourg* of Pétion-Ville, where my grandmother lived. I could stand here at any time of day and see my life passing before my eyes: father putting on his shoes to walk to the cane factory where he kept the books; brothers and sisters pulling each other's hair. I don't see myself, ever. Perhaps this is because I was always standing in the same place, observing, waiting. It took a lifetime of watching and waiting. Mother and father passed away and I was the one who, at twenty-one, made the arrangements to have them buried in the cemetery, not far from the Palace, in the sector for people who could pay for their burial plots and even have their full names engraved on their gravestones. Father had saved all his life to prepare properly for the days he would walk on the other side, depriving himself even of trips to Cap-Haitien to see his brother and family during the long years of the Occupation. He was, though, not so much concerned with the afterlife (I don't know that he believed in such things) but on how he would be lowered into the ground: the right suit, dress, shoes; coffins made-to-order and trimmed with velvet.

A year later, Gustave came into my life. I was wearing the traditional black vestments of grief, yet he still noticed me. It seemed that life began the very moment he approached me at the market, to point out that there were better avocados than the two I had chosen and placed in my mesh bag. He held up an avocado the size of a small grapefruit, its green skin glowing like a live thing, and placed it in the palm of my hand. He said it had been hiding at the back of the pile, just waiting for me. Some things, he said, are worth searching for. Then he tipped his straw hat towards me and smiled before going on his way, calling out to a paperboy to bring around his car. From that day on, Gustave eased himself into my heart, as if fate had brought him to me. And he stayed there for fifteen years, until the day he died in a cell in Fort-Dimanche, of hunger they say, because he protested for a minimum wage the day a minister of Papa Doc's came home from buying a mansion in the South of France. This time, I did not make the arrangements for laying him to rest. Gustave had a wife.

I sat in the pew at the back of the Church during his final mass and watched her still back. I knew she could feel the heat of my eyes against her smooth skin the colour of walnuts fallen from the trees. Her long black hair was swept up in a Spanish roll (they say she was a Dominican), exposing the long and narrow neck which would have rested in his hands on the nights he did not come to me. She wore a veil and I never saw the features which lay exposed in her children's faces, who otherwise looked so much like mine – but lighter in skin-tone – the roundness of their chins betraying their father. I left there with a stone in my heart as she broke down crying at the sight of his ashen face. He would never smile for us again, telling jokes about the newspaper business and how corrupt the world had become as he counted how many copies of the *Nouveau Jour* had been sold in the capital that day. That night while our four children slept, conceived in the heat of passionate embraces and a flurry of unkept promises, I began to pray to the Virgin Mary for strength. I was again a woman alone, only now even more lonely, for where before there had been only emptiness and yearning, now there was the knowledge of love and its loss eating away at my spirit like a worm.

He came to me some thirty years after his death with the face of a young man ready for a new adventure. I felt the familiar wavy hair so soft beneath my fingers. And the moustache spreading like crows' wings across his thin lips which I had wanted him to shave off, but he wouldn't, saying he would look like a child. Really, he was afraid of letting his lips show and I was afraid to tell him that they were even smaller hidden under the hairs. I liked the moustache after a while, called it *Monsieur* whenever it came near me and tickled my cheeks. Gustave looked like a playboy with his slicked-back hair and tailored vests, narrow ties with pins made of solid gold. His family had emigrated from Martinique to become part of the new Haiti the Americans had been promising to bring back to life in the early 1920s. Haiti, then as now, was for sale, and Gustave's family bought in. But he had ideals, Gustave, built a small empire out of a leftist newspaper which always managed to speak in code so not as to be shut down. I listened to Gustave and his dreams and watched them turn to dust, as he accepted tracts of land and visas to America to keep certain people's names out of the news. And I listen to him now as he reaches out to me, as if he has just come home from a trip abroad, his pockets filled with candy for the children, a broach or bracelet for me. He is still spouting the same rainbows and streets paved with freedom. I turn away from him, feeling the weight of my seventy-five years pulling on a body I no longer recognize as my own, the thick ankles brimming over the clasps of my leather sandals like frothing milk left too long over an open flame.

It is in this moment of turning away that I begin to see at the back, in front, and all around me. I sit in the kitchen with the flies crawling over the fruit in the hand-hollowed mahogany bowl Gustave brought from a village in the mountains to ask for forgiveness for something I would no longer remember were it not for the bowl staring me in the face. He had gone on a holiday with his wife and I was sitting on my anger, looking out through the open door down the dirt path leading to the main road, watching stray dogs scratching themselves against the wire fence. It was summer and the children were home, playing in their rooms or in the yard, coming to me every few minutes or so to ask when Papi would return to play with them. I would turn them back to their books, their games of dice, the skipping rope moored to the verandah, too afraid to speak lest my anger spill out like scalding steam. Staring at that bowl, I remember my anger as if it was yesterday. That bowl whispered secrets I did not want to hear.

It had taken me seventy-four years to look at my life the way one looks at the peel of a mango, making sure that all of its flesh has been stripped clean, before throwing it away. I remembered my children when they were small, their uniqueness, their simple joy. There is something about the ease children have in knowing who they are – until day by day they lose that assurance – that I treasured in each of mine. For years, it did not matter that some were girls and some were boys. They played with each other and were the best of friends. They were generous with their toys, their food, their ears. They seemed to know instinctively that love was one of those things that you could only get by giving it away. I did not worry about them. I delighted in them. They seemed so happy, I was so happy; I forgot to pay them attention. I worked long hours sewing and cleaning for the women up and down the street – hours so long that sometimes I woke in the dark and slept in the light. The older children began to take care of the younger ones once they started going to school and this was when the fighting began. I discovered I had two boys and two girls – two boys who wanted to win like their father and two girls who thought all was lost and looked on me with pity. But, as I say, my days were no longer days and I did not notice these changes – at least I made no attempt to see where they would lead. It may have been that I was waiting for Gustave to leave his wife, something he was unlikely to do. It is painful to look back and forward and every which way to find out that your aloneness could have been prevented.

Two of my four children went away from me, leaving holes I did not know how to fill. One, Léo, a businessman, took after his father, enjoying life but forgetting the dreams of freedom. The other, Ralph, an intellectual, stewed in despair until all he could do was spew hatred. He flew away to France to study and never returned. The girls, Jacqueline and Maude, like me, lived their lives behind their husbands, denying that anything was wrong when their men did not come home for whole weeks at a time, denying any resemblance between their children and those they saw playing in the streets in the next town or village. Perhaps they thought they were the lucky ones since they had rings on their fingers and their men presented themselves at their sides in church every Sunday. I see it all so clearly now: how they were too afraid to step out of their houses, the way they wore the latest fashions to hide their fear, puffing on *Gauloises* as if all that smoke wouldn't catch up with them one day. And they ignore their children as I see now *I* ignored them. I would like to think that my daughters' negligence is the more cruel since they do not work and they are married, but I do not know that this is true.

I watched my grandchildren grow sullen after their first years of delight at hearing their voices answered in the middle of the night by women they thought were their mothers but turn out to be hired help. Some of the children grew up yelling at these women as if they were stray dogs, whenever they wanted a cool drink or a shirt pressed for an evening out. And I was surprised to see the women accept these voices full of venom – this because I felt that I was one of these women, a laundry woman, a working woman. My heart was full of worms when I saw them, adults and children alike, locked in these battles as if they had no choice.

Maude, my older daughter, has had little to do with me since the day her third and last born began school; then she no longer needed me to take care of the little ones when she wanted to gossip with the neighbour wives. Jacqueline is different. I believe it matters to her that her daughter knows me. For her, I am not just an unpaid carer. She sends her daughter to me on Sundays with Léo, after or before mass. I can see how my daughter and granddaughter are so much alike: Josèphe is always hand-in-hand with another little girl, Désirée. They bob together like the two small corks they set floating in a basin, imagining they are ships out at sea. When Jacqueline was small she was this way with Désirée's mother, Rosaline. I would forget that Rosaline was not my daughter since she was stumbling over my feet from morning to night, playing in the yard, eating at our table, laughing with her mouth full at Jacqueline, and returning home only after I had impressed upon her her mother's loneliness at seeing her gone for so long. Jacqueline would walk Rosaline two doors down in the light of the moon and I remember thinking that this friend-ship would last a lifetime, and it has. Rosaline no longer lives down the road; she too is married and has risen like the dust of these roads to meet a fresher air. Yet, she remains close to Jacqueline and sends her daughter along on Sundays to me; her own mother is no longer with us. Josèphe and Désirée play in my yard like their mothers before them, though unaware that they are repeating the past. I treat them as if they are sisters so that when they are older they will remember they have each other, even at times when it will seem that they have nothing else.

Sometimes, Léo brings Alphonse with them and I play along as if I do not know that the boy is his own son, not just a playmate for the girls. I know this as clearly as I see the way his ears curve away from his head like porcelain handles on milk pitchers, as Gustave's did before him. And I see the way Alphonse carries himself as if the whole world might someday bow before him as

Léo does when he doubts his abilities. He is my grandson and I greet him like the girls, with kisses on both cheeks and oranges to take back to his little room in the cavern below his father's house. I suspect he knows who he is. And I wonder if it is always this way for the children who are not claimed, if at the backs of their heads they have the same eyes I have grown and the knowledge that others try to keep things from them like sugary sweets that will rot the teeth.

On the days when all three of them are here with me, I show them how my mother baked bread in the oven and I make the dishes I never bothered to teach my sons and daughters. I show them how to kill chickens with their bare hands – so they will know how to survive, if it ever comes to that. I show them how to loosen the feathers from the skin by plunging the carcass into a pan of hot water. I make the chicken dish simple, so that they will know that life can be just that easy, not hidden beneath fattening sauces and bland flavours. I pile their plates high with rice and kidney beans, flavoured only with pepper, salt and two dried bay leaves. I pile high so they will remember that love can be like this, a bounty, and they must never be ashamed to give themselves more. I show them how to share the squares of *douces* I make with cane syrup for dessert, so that they will know that what is special must not be squandered. Still, this is not enough.

They leave the door of my house – which I painted a bright yellow so that it will stick in their minds when they go from here – my granddaughter far away to Canada where I know the cold sinks into her skin like a poison and frosts her heart. They leave here and they see things I could not bear to see until Gustave came to tell me that my time was coming soon, too soon.

Outside the door I have made so bright, to replace the unhappiness spreading through their minds like cobwebs, they see children like themselves who have nothing, whose faces are streaked with days of dust. They look into those eyes and I know they begin to doubt themselves and I know that one day they will turn against those children or turn against themselves. I grow listless with plans to plot answers to the questions they find in the brown eyes so much like their own. They return to me with the shadows of their encounters lodged in their pupils, like pieces of sand

14

blown there, warnings of storms to come. It takes me back to my own childhood days.

I remember holding my father's hand as we watched *vodou* ceremonies in the dark of a village miles from home, and how the beating of the drums seemed to flow from the earth to his feet and through his body to our hands. We watched the figures dressed in white with painted faces drawing the *vèvès* with cornmeal on the ground to Erzulie. I recognized street vendors among the robed figures: the women who stand by the side of the shacks in the *lakou-foumi*, the men with scarred faces smoking in little groups on porches bleached with decay. I remember this as if it were yesterday and my father taking me away from the ceremony as the bodies begin to dance against one another as if the last judgment had come and the judgment has been good. It strikes me now that my mother was never there with us, watching and listening.

It is here that I learned to pray Metrès Ezili rather than to her twin image, the Virgin Marie. Now I turn to her not for forgiveness and hope, but to ask that strength be given to my grandchildren, even the one who does not have my blood flowing through her veins. I do not want them to turn into monsters or hollow versions of themselves, like my own children, or, like me, blind old women who must have spirits appear before they are willing to see that there is something wrong with the world beyond them.

Now I see things I have never seen before, that stun me into despair and I finally understand why my youngest son left, never to return, filling his head with nonsense and writing essays in a French I could never understand – so unlike the cadences of our *créole* which made me so free and full of talk in the days when I thought everything was all right. Even now, language is the barrier I cannot pull down between the children and myself. Léo insists that the girls spend their weekends in Port-au-Prince unlearning all the things I want to teach them. I talk proverb-talk so that they will be wiser than those around them. I say to them after a good meal: *Sa-k nan vant ou sé li-k pa ou*. If they are eating too quickly, I say: *Trò présé pa fè jou louvri!* This way, they know that the good that is in them is all they need to survive. They learn to appreciate the small things in life like sunsets and wind and the new buds of flowering trees. But sometimes it all seems like throwing water into a lake the way they come back to me, speaking this foreign tongue and affecting new ways I cannot understand whatever way I turn them, up or down, forwards or backwards, like a chicken roasting on a pit which is not yet quite done. Then, all I can say to them is: *Apa sé vini ouap vini? Oua ouè!* And our visits end in anger and the shadows of goodbyes.

I begin to be careless after I recognize the change in them. I use the wrong measures for the dishes I prepare and they taste bitter and overcooked. I forget to turn down the heat when the oil begins to splutter on the stove and the room spins around me like a top. Everything is changing and I fear that there is nothing I can teach these children which will change the course of their lives.

They are wilting before my eyes and I know what is happening to them, though they do not speak to me as they used to when they believed I could keep them safe. Almost twenty years ago now, my granddaughter came back to me one Sunday, walking like a small bird that has been brought down from the blue skies with a sharp stone. Now she stumbles over small things and is afraid of noises. I am filled with such anger that I have seen nothing, done nothing until now. Someone has turned her from a free, open child to one who is afraid, closed, unhappy. That same Sunday, I realized too that Désirée walked as if she had discovered that joy and pain could be paired like the blades of scissors, as if she was ready to put away her dolls and jump-ropes, thinking that to leap into the adult world would save her from the loneliness her mother and father had placed in her since the day she was born. Why is it that I did not sit down with each of these girls and have them spill out these secrets, unburden their fears? Why have I not taught them to love themselves, to nurture their bodies and their minds like *douces*? I carry this wound like the scar on my stomach from the burn of spilled oil, a caution against my own silences.

I cannot forgive those who have turned my heart, these children, into pieces of burning coal. When Jacqueline came to me with her right eye swollen shut, red like a ripe tomato, I tell her – this daughter of mine who smokes her cigarettes as if they are pieces of exotic chocolate, who wears her miniskirts as if she

16

is still childless, twenty-years old and looking for her life – to leave her husband and these shores for the continent. I had heard things about the continent from Gustave. It is there that all hope resides, the riches, the possibilities, the freedom to make and unmake yourself as many times as your life can take. There they will be free of these men in blue, some so young they can't even grow a moustache, who scorn them and belittle them and mutilate their bodies. Things have changed, I told her; do not repeat the mistakes I have made. My daughter listens as I tell her never to bring her child back to this world. I will never see Josèphe again, except for in letters and dreams, but this is the price I am willing to pay so that she may be a child a little longer, not having to make the choices I let my own children struggle through – as if at the age of seven they could take care of themselves. Of course, I'd had little choice then, making ends meet like Jacqueline had to do once she landed in Canada, cleaning houses for a living. I wonder if she lived as lonely as I had done, living lonely for Gustave who was forever absent.

I know I have done the right thing when I hear about Céleste Dominique's son, Delphi, dying in a rally in the mountains. It was a man his own age who pulled the trigger in his face as he walked by carrying a placard with the words: *Ayiti, sé tè tout moun.* They did not realize they had turned him into the land itself, that the people would make him a hero for speaking his mind at a time when loving your country and the people in it is like asking the angel of death to take you home.

My granddaughter grows into a woman far away from me. I hear her voice calling to me from time to time and I answer by sending her, in little boxes, pieces of myself and the life I wish she could have here. I send her the jewellery Gustave gave me in the days he came to my house and our children as if there was no other place in the world he could be. I send her pictures of me when I was young and ready for the world to tell me all its secrets. I send her the silverware set I never completed in all the years I was with her grandfather. He had brought back some of the pieces from a trip to Santo Domingo. I had waited for him to realize that if I'd had the whole set I would have felt like I belonged to him, but he never did and I added a piece here and there every few years –

sometime around our anniversary which we celebrated by opening a bottle of rum and making a punch so the children could have small sips and fall asleep before we made love as we had done in the years before each of them was born. These small miracles in my life I did not treasure until it was far too late. I tell her everything is fine but my life will soon end and that she must learn to be strong for herself.

We cannot talk on the phone. No, it isn't the cost that keeps us silent, speaking only to each other in our minds, it's the clicking on the line and the murmurs of breathing telling you that you are not alone. We cannot take chances. But this silence keeps me from having to tell her how things have gone from bad to worse, from poverty to chaos, from hope to anarchy. I cannot write the long, flowery phrases her uncle could have written her in his cryptic, philosophical French, but I tell her I love her by telling her to pray. I scribble quotes from the New Testament because it is the only Holy Book I have and write them in cards bought at the grocery store that are faded with age. I want her to understand that she cannot kill her life before it has begun. After I send these things across the waters and into the vast emptiness of America, I sit quiet in the porch of my house, the paint along the boards of the doorframe peeling away in long slivers of pale yellow, and I wait.

I think of my mother as she stood beside the oven, looking up into the sky, hoping that each mouth she fed would feast upon life without cruelty and make this land hum with the love she kneaded into the loaves of bread now rising and turning a golden brown in the heat.

My secret eyes fill my soul with sorrow as I feel the weight in my body growing lighter with every sway of the *dodine* creaking beneath me.

And I wait for Gustave to come for me again, sheltering in his hands the promises of my younger heart, beckoning me homewards at long and final last.

PART ONE

MY STORY

CHAPTER ONE

I found out when I was twelve years old that there were people all over the world who worshipped the Heavenly Mother. They formed the Cult of the Virgin, or what is sometimes called the Cult of Mary. I drafted myself into the order secretly one day, after listening to our parish priest denounce those of us who could not tell the difference between the worship of the spirit and the worship of icons. Father Michael stopped his speech to take from under his cloak a square of hand-stitched fabric to wipe his perspiring moustache. He told us that icon worshippers were under the worst kind of delusion: they could not tell solid matter from spirit, pieces of wood from electric charges sent from above. Representations of the gods were artifice, he said, his stomach heaving in front of him and butting against the pulpit so that the light above his papers quivered. He lost his train of thought and began to speak of missionary work in Africa. His brother was a missionary, he told us, a lost lamb who believed it was his duty to feed the body before nourishing the spirit. Father Michael shook his head again and wiped his face on his sleeve. He looked out over us. We were a meagre lot strewn about like potato peels amongst the pews. I looked back up at him, a man the size of three Haitian men rolled into one plump body: how could I believe anything he said?

But I believed in the Virgin Mary. In my grandmother's house when I was a child, there was a picture of her on a shelf in an alcove in the wall of her kitchen, facing the stove and the hanging basket which held her fresh-baked bread. The back of the shelf was translucent glass in front of which Grandmother had placed a picture of the Virgin painted on a block of wood. Mary's head is bent downwards: her face, a thin tear-shape the deep purplish brown of an apple seed; her eyes mere lines of black to show that she is deep in thought. She is cloaked in blue and wears a gold bejewelled crown, gold bangles and silver bracelets around her delicate wrists. One hand is turned upwards as if shielding her from a hot sun, the other is turned out towards her audience like a dancer asking for a partner in the moonlight. There is a ring on every finger. A candle of oil burns in a green earthen jar hiding the mounds of her breasts pierced through by a dagger thrust into her heart, the sacred heart of our Mother-Saviour. My saviour. My mother. Grandmother ends all her prayers with the words: "*Mé'ci Bondye. Mé'ci Sen Marie. Gen pitye sou nou é gadé tout pitit mwen andedan kè ou.*" Then, she places a gardenia fresh from the yard by the jar and watches the icon until the Virgin Mary smiles by letting the wick in the oil flicker.

For years, I believed that the Holy Mother could save me from the world. I prayed to her as I went to sleep and every morning when my eyes opened to greet a new day. These days, it gets harder and harder to rise from bed and believe that anything good might happen, but I make the sign of the cross in the shower and tell her that I will do anything to be happy just once in this life, anything to be free of my past.

★ ★ ★ ★

I walk out of the house into the cold gusts of prairie winds to catch the bus which will take me to the University. Snow banks are piled high by the side of the road, brown sand disrupting the white ribbons spreading out across the quiet fields. Hay bails left to disintegrate with the melting snow in the far off spring peak out in yellow patches from the dense whiteness as if pleading for rescue. I walk on, head wrapped in a multicoloured scarf from the Hudson's Bay Company I bought with baby-sitting money a month ago, hoping it would lift my spirits. The Red River is on the other side of the housing park where I live. In the summer, all the kids used to bike there, along the trails hidden among the maple and fir trees whose roots were fed by the waters we

21

polluted with our Bazooka gum wrappers and dirty Band-Aids. We called them the monkey trails, hoping to turn them into the wild Congo. I never thought much about it then, our use of language. But I think about it now, everyday that I have to walk down this sidewalk and away from the house where I choose to hide my life, because I think I am really awake in another life, a better one, somewhere in the sun with my grandmother, sitting under a swaying palm tree protecting us with its shade.

I walk with my coat wrapped tightly around me. The coat is grey and bloated with feathers plucked from birds I suspect are endangered. It keeps me warm and cold at the same time. I wonder if people looking out their windows see only a coat walking down the street past the field and the neighbourhood recreation centre, past the railroad tracks. I eye these tracks suspiciously every time I lift a foot to step over the thick metal guides and examine them for grooves made by the sharp wheels of the three o'clock morning train. Today, as every day, I stand on one of the wooden sleepers and look down the tracks to see the point at which they meet and ask for signs that are never sent me. I think of the Willa Cather story, "Paul's Case" that we are reading in literature class. I understood Paul and his interrupted life that went nowhere he wanted to go. Cather wrote: "When the right moment came, he jumped." And I had wanted to know when Paul knew it was the right moment to end his life as the train barrelled towards him; seconds after that moment he wanted to take it back, redraw the contours of his existence. I stand in the middle of the railroad tracks and try to imagine that final moment of being struck by the oncoming engine, the blood spreading across the snow like a fine mist.

When I see the bus rounding the corner from by the Anglican Church two blocks away, I run all the way down to my stop. Breathless, I step up the slippery rubber mats sprinkled with chips of salt to melt away the snow each of us brings into the bus clinging to the edges of our boots. Tomorrow, I think, tomorrow I will wake before the train has time to blare its warning horn and I will stand there, in the middle of the tracks, ready to meet it. I would never again have to think that the way the flatness of the sky meets the land is so much like the sea, and that if I could fly away,

I would. Never have to think I was in the wrong place. Never have to wake to the smoke of my breath suspended in the air because everything is frozen except my brain, which keeps asking me, over and over again: How did I get here? How do I find my way home again?

* * * *

October 1988

Dear Josèphe,

Comment vas-tu? Why haven't you written? It's been months and months and I've written you twice now with no answer. Is everything all right? I hope you are O.K. and that you are meeting lots of new people at the University. Here it doesn't look like there will be a chance for us to go back. I was two courses away from getting my certificate in accounting. Now, it may be never. What matters is that we keep having our meetings with the youth leaders all over the country. Whatever they tell you, don't believe it; we are alive with hope.

I met someone at the last meeting. He believes in justice and makes long, flowery speeches in front of every one. He has no fear. And, of course, he is very handsome and tall. All the girls think he is a great catch but Charles says he only has eyes for me. Can you believe it? In any case, I don't want you to worry about us, to concentrate on your studies. Everything you learn will set you free. Then maybe you can come back here and help us? We'll need young people to lead when everything falls apart. It's bound to happen sooner or later. How long can people live in fear? How long can the military knock market women down on the street corners as they try to sell their wilting flowers and meat festooned with hungry flies? At night, the guns go off dozens at a time and I swear I can hear every bullet as it lands in pillars of wood or burrows into the wrinkled flesh of a man who is old enough to have seen the Americans come and go with their filthy green jeeps.

We work with some of the radio-rebels. You must have

heard of them. They are the ones who work on short wave and AM, moving frequencies as much as possible and whenever they are found out. This way, they can communicate all over the island, into the deepest reaches of the mountains. We have spent nights on the airwaves sending messages from village to village, using music more than words. Between each song we say what must be said: "Tomorrow, we will see the dawning of a new day" or "Today, all the children have been fed" followed by a choice cut from the U.S. or France. We have to choose local music carefully because almost every artist here is marked either as a subversive or a party-player and we don't want to contribute to someone's murder. Sometimes I want it all to be over, but most of the time I feel that I am part of history. I wouldn't want to have been born anywhere else, would you? I really do want to know how you are.

I would call you but you know how useless that would be. Please answer this letter. You don't know how I worry and wait, looking in the mailbox even after Bella has brought in the day's mail after she sets the table for luncheon. My father is away again and I am staying with your aunt and uncle until Mother is ready to mother again. She is with one of her boyfriends in Martinique.

Did you know that your Uncle Léo has a room filled with bags of keys of every colour and shape? He must have the key to the presidential palace somewhere in there. Charles wants to rob the place but I won't let him, because of you. It's not our fault we have such a bad seed in the family, is it? I did take one key from the room when no one was in the house; it's the key to the room we shared when we were children. I want you to keep it and bring it back with you the day you return. Will you do that? I know you will. Write me soon. All your news. Don't leave anything out, and tell me how cold it is the day you read this.

Avec amour,
Désirée

I fold and unfold the letter. It is beginning to tear around the edges even though I keep it safely tucked in its envelope on the days when I can't bear to see Désirée's French cursive hand trying to reach me across the land and water that keeps us apart. I finger the stamps marked "République d'Haiti" festooned with bright outlines of birds and fish I don't recognize any more. The letters come every few months and one by one I fail to answer them.

I haven't taken pen to paper for at least two years. It was '87 or '88 and time seemed to have gone crazy, beyond control. Haiti was in the news everyday since the coup ousted the Duvaliers. Every exiled Haitian has this picture etched in her or his mind, whether they saw it on television or in a newspaper: the steel grey Mercedes (or was it something far more expensive?) speeding past a shouting mob; Michèle with a white turban wrapped round her head, looking into the distance as if this were all very normal, dragging on her four-inch long Gauloises – which were probably as long as her stiletto heels (which must have been blood-red, hidden behind the door). And then the screen turned black, the Duvaliers' destination was announced and they were gone. The day I stopped writing was not that day. Not that day exactly. It was the beginning of my need for silence, for utter stillness. And yet, it seems to me now that it was then that all the memories began to flood my body like a fever.

The day I decided to stop writing completely was the day I sat in front of the television with a microwave dinner to watch the news to see Eric, a boy ten years older than me, whom I had known in childhood, driving a coal truck down an unmarked road from Pétion-Ville to the capital. It was unmistakably him. There are some people you need encounter only once in a lifetime never to forget them. It's something about their eyes' deep coldness or unexpected warmth. It's something about the way they look at you and empty their venom or their love into you and your soul carries the imprint of that look for the rest of your life. Eric was one of those people for me and I watched his eyes fill with terror as the crowd began hauling him out of the truck's cab. The mob, protesting years of death by terror in a square nearby, took hold of Eric's shirt, which was frayed about the edges, a coral pink. Stones were being thrown at him, at his truck. They were like the ones you read about in the Bible, dug out of riverbanks and carried on mule-back to build houses for the wealthy in the Egyptian hills. Rocks to build. Rocks to kill. These were rocks that had to be held with both hands and thrown from above the head. I watched as they struck him in the face, opening long gashes in the soft flesh, smashing his breastbone, forcing him to his knees which buckled beneath him. I watched Eric fall into a pool of his own blood, teeth breaking against the pavement. Then he seemed to be nothing more than a small dot in the crowd which flowed over him like a frothing tide. I wanted to protect him and save him, and yet I also wanted to join in with the crowd, raise my fists to pummel him into the ground.

The camera showed the last moments of his life, the stillness of the ripped shirt against his chest, the clumps of hair torn out in handfuls lying beside his inert body and the wild look in his eyes rolling back into his head. The announcer, seemingly amazed at the violence of the demonstration, declared over and over: "The man, Eric Laurier, was suspected of being a member of the notorious secret police, the Tons-Tons Mack-oots."

I wanted those words to be reason enough to put pen to paper. But I chose silence: there are stories I can never tell. Letters I will never write home.

★ ★ ★ ★

November 1989

Dearest Jo,

You have become silent. Why? I think about you every day and wonder where you are and if life in Canada is treating you well. Charles talks of leaving this place and taking me to Montréal. Have you been there? He says there are a lot of Haitians there and we wouldn't have to speak any English at all if we didn't want to. Wouldn't that be nice? Have you ever thought about moving to Québec? It could be the saving grace for you. But who am I to give you advice? I don't even know if this letter is reaching you. Maybe you have moved from 403 Southview Apartments in Winnipeg. I try to imagine you living by yourself and

26

wonder how you do it. Really, I would like to know how you do it.

Charles and I are planning to leave the hills behind and join the people on the streets. There are bands of homeless children in Port-au-Prince. I say children because they are young, but many of them are like us, wanting to make a change in the country. We would like to join them. You don't think it's too late for me, do you? I worry about it, you see, because I still dream of escaping to Paris and having a carefree life strolling along the cobbled streets and buying Rodier sweaters whenever I can afford to from the real couturier. And then, I remember those children we used to see when we went out to Kenscoff for our days of fun with Tonton Léo. They were no different from us except that they had no money to buy food and no one to care for them. We had our parents even though they kept forgetting about us and leaving us to our own devices. But we had Grandmother, always. She isn't well you know. You must have a lot of classes to keep track of and things to do, but write her a card when you have the chance. Just to let her know you haven't forgotten. Write soon.

How cold is it today?

Love,

D.

★ ★ ★ ★

December 1990

Dear Désirée,

This is a letter I won't send you, I know that. But writing a few things down on paper will make me feel as if something has been said. You keep asking me how cold it is in the winter. Did you know that the corner of Portage and Main, where traffic converges from all parts of the city in front of the Bank of Montreal, is the coldest place in Western Canada when the windchill is factored into the equation? As low as minus fifty degrees Celsius. That means that your skin freezes in less than a second if exposed. Which also means that you never stand on the corner to look anyone in the face and everyone is so busy getting to their destination. . . I've looked for Rodier sweaters and they don't sell them here, though I hear that knock-offs have been shipped to the States since the mid-70s.

I do have a lot to tell you. I just don't now where to begin, or where I'll end if I start. You and Charles seem very brave to me and I wish I could join you as you set off on your new lives. My life at the University is hopeless. I don't know what relevance any of these classes have to anything. I wrote a paper last week on the ethics of suicide and how religion keeps us from loving people fully and then demonizes them when they lose faith in the world. If I committed suicide I would be a *lâche*, a coward. Why is it that I can't figure out what to do with myself? For us? For Haïti? Why am I so afraid to do anything?

I watched Eric die on the tele today and I saw Tonton Léo's house when they were talking about the Macoutes. It's a good thing you're leaving soon. Who knows what kind of mess you could be in for. I love you very much and I wish we could go back to a time when things weren't so upside down. My mother tells me stories about growing up in the country and how she had her own horse and dogs; how they weren't poor but they weren't rich either and everyone helped everyone else. Where has that world gone? My friend Sara's father talks this same way about growing up in the Dakotas and I wonder if it's not an epidemic that has hit the whole world, except that in Haiti every illness is always worse – always misery turning into death. I wish you had been my sister and not just my cousin, that you could tell me now what I should do with my life. Every day I'm surprised that I am still alive because, inside, it seems as if I died long ago. I live in this country of immigrants and throw away the food I cannot eat as if it doesn't matter that somewhere in a bidonville of Port-au-Prince people would fight like animals over every morsel. I live as an immigrant in this country, and cry when I see even men like Eric stoned to death, because there is no justice in our country, only streams of pain.

I end the letter there and fold it away with Désirée's. I carry the bundle in my book bag to and from the University, as if I might run into someone who'll be able to decipher them for me, tell me what it is that keeps me from mailing my response, what it is that makes me want my separation from home to be absolute.

★ ★ ★ ★

The Film Studies class is the only one in which I can breathe. We sit in an auditorium with a floor made sticky over the years from smuggled cans of soft drinks spilling in the dark as the films are shown. There is a sign on the door: NO FOOD. NO DRINK. For years the students have ignored it, but the *gardiens* haven't caught on. Or, if they have, they pretend that the floors are as pristine as those of the libraries up the stairs. We sit in large cushiony seats covered in worn red velvet. I slip into the same seat every time, four rows up and two spaces in so I can make a quick exit if I need to. I keep my coat wrapped around me because central heating hasn't been installed in this small room where we all watch each other like birds of prey. The teacher is a graduate student drafted in to teach us the basics after our professor decided he had better things to do – like roaming around France watching grapes being turned into wine. And who could blame him, we think, sitting in our chairs like stuffed tomatoes, waiting for the rolls of film to be unwound so we can escape from ourselves and this seedy room into imaginary landscapes.

"How are you liking the class?"

The voice belongs to Georges Deschamps, a transfer student from the French college in St. Boniface. His skin is permanently tanned, as if he has just come off a plane from a faraway place. His eyes smile even when he is being serious, discussing the impact of silent film on modern consciousness or the propagandic significance of documentary film in the Third World. He has laugh lines at the corner of each eye, though I have never heard him laugh.

"Are you liking the class?" His voice wavers like a crow cawing in the *mornes* near the South coast of Haiti. His hair is thick and jet black and I wonder where his ancestors came from and where he got his green-blue eyes. I know he is left-handed from watching him doodle his way through the screening of the original Disney version of *Pinocchio*. I know he likes the mysteries of lighting from the way he leaned forward to watch *The Maltese Falcon* until his chin came to rest against the seat in front of him.

"I like it all right."

"So, does that mean you like it like it, or you just put up with it?"

"I like it like it."

"O.K.," he seems encouraged, "which film have you liked best?"

I don't know how to answer. If I say I liked an obscure Italian classic, I will seem pretentious and if I choose a Hollywood comedy I will seem flighty. "Well," I say, measuring the next words out carefully as if I was handing out Valentines in grade school, afraid of someone laughing at the hearts I'd cut out of pink card at the kitchen table the night before, writing "Have a great ♥ day", in a shaky hand twenty times over: "I just like to sit in the dark and get inside the characters. It really doesn't matter in which film."

Georges has a surprised look on his face and I wonder what he's thinking about me. I stare at the screen and hope he'll turn around as he usually does, ignoring everyone but the lecturer and his pad of yellow paper. I don't know what it means that he has made this effort. I wonder why, after weeks of this class, he has decided to reach out to me.

The room dims into darkness and the screen flickers with movement. The larger-than-life figures move in slow motion behind Georges' head and still he does not turn away from me. Instead, he extends his hand and introduces himself, as if a formal introduction was needed before we could embark on a joint chapter in our lives he has already begun to write.

★ ★ ★ ★

A few months after meeting Georges, I no longer stop at the railroad tracks in the morning to wonder about their point of convergence. I have my own now and I hurry towards him as if he might disappear if I let any time go by. But Georges is there, waiting at the bus stop in front of the dorms even when the windchill brings the temperature down as low as that at Portage and Main. He brings me surprises, sometimes a book but most often photographs he takes in the afternoons when the light begins to fade. He dreams about making films. Sometimes we go out to the farms in the village-towns of Borden and St. Pierre and he strolls around with his Super 8 camera, framing objects I learned to ignore as my family settled into city life and turned its back on nature – objects like ploughs and horse bits and oil lamps. He talks big talk, my Grandmother would say, but I don't mind. His voice keeps me buoyed up through my loneliness, until the emptiness inside me begins to be filled. I forget to pray to Virgin Mother, as if my troubles are over.

I haven't realized yet that one can't rush into the future without having looked the past in the face. I know that facing the past would be like holding up a mirror to myself and seeing the pain hidden there, behind the skin still recovering from the scars of adolescence, in the eyes round with anticipation and deep as wells, in the hair pulled back tightly to tame its springy curls, in the rose-pink lips closed against white teeth to suppress any sign of the happiness which might be lurking there: a life half-lived, cut-off at the roots. Not wanting to face myself, I leap into Georges' dreams of making a documentary about surviving in the Prairies and listen to his stories of growing up without a father in Brandon, Manitoba – a city I have only seen once but liked the look of because it looked so American from the back seat of the car when I went there one bright summer afternoon with my parents to picnic. The billboards speeding by the side of the road announced the first Burger King north of the border and an open-air cinema with a snack bar. I imagine Georges there, dissatisfied, looking for a way out as he sped through the streets angrily on a motorbike, like a miniature James Dean looking for a fight and a woman to love (me, of course, waiting to be carried away in a yellow chiffon dress at the edge of town).

"I want you to be honest now. As honest as you can be." Georges opens up his portfolio in my lap and there is picture after picture of sunsets and old buildings falling into ruin, and me in my green parka in the middle of a country road. "I've never seen you smile like that before," he says.

It's true. My chin is still with delight as my lips open wide into a smile and my mind is dancing with soft thoughts of that day when we sat in the car and Georges took my frozen hands out of my wool mittens to warm them in his hands. I reach out to touch the smoothness of his cheek, so different from the stubbly beards that scratched my forehead those nights I stayed out dancing and drinking in the University Pub trying to forget life, as if morning would not come and bring with it a hollow, painful pounding in the temples.

"They're wonderful," I say, just to be saying something that will carry my voice out of me and into the air between us, releasing my unspoken desires to be close to him.

"Really," he says, pleased, "I worried about the light."

"No," I smile, "It's just right. So very right."

We fall back onto the cushions and hear the book of photographs hitting the ground with an empty thud. His hands find my body and a warmth stretches out from between my legs to the layer of cells directly beneath the surface of my skin straining to meet his.

I hear the sound of paper buckling. My mouth envelops the half moon of his tongue. His taste is like bursts of unexpected joy against my palate. I keep my eyes open to see his laugh lines folding into each other like flower petals closing over one another against the falling dew. I hold onto the muscles of his back as if to anchor off a rocky shore and breath in the air filtered through his body. I float below him like a fishing boat along Cap Rose facing Cuba, where Fidel gave shoes to the children while ours drifted off to sleep, never to waken. Then, the inevitable shedding of clothes. The warmth disappears, turns into fear. I see Eric's hands seeking me out, tearing me to pieces; Eric's face sneering into mine. The smells of faraway erupt between George's body and mine: the half-rotting softness of avocados and mangoes: Eric's sweat falling against my neck; chickens fighting each other in a square pen. And pain. And finally, I am crying and I imagine my grandmother's soft strong arms sweeping me up gently and cradling me to sleep.

I wake to look into George's laugh lines. They are taut. They remind me of the leathery skin of servants who toil under an unforgiving sun to fan the well-to-do mistress of the house who waits to be rescued, rather than rise on her own, from the reclining chair where she is installed behind the high walls that keep her from the world and the world from her. But I am not one of these women. He is not a servant. Why think such things? I am drowning in images of a faraway world. A world which is now a fossilized caricature. I realize that memories cling to the brain like moss to the bark of aged trees, but still I cannot convince myself to tell Georges about the country of my mind, the secret place where all my nightmares have come to rest.

It is then that I begin to write these pages, deep into the night, filling piece after piece of scrap paper with my memories, as distant and unclear as they are. It doesn't matter to me how it all comes out. It is like vomiting up a virus that has weakened your muscles and clouded the sharp, clear pattern of your thoughts. It is like freeing some part of me too long mute.

★ ★ ★ ★

June 1990

Allo Josèphe,

Comment ça vas? I write you from the Big Apple. I have come to America finally and I will come find you sometime if that is all right. O.K.? I hear nothing about you all these years. I carry letters for you from D. There not being a lot, I send them along. She is not doing well, not well at all. She maybe gone *loco*, you know? Voudou. It does that to some people. Sends them on all kinds of wild goose chases. I don't get mixed up in all that. You know me. Playing safe with what I've got. Anyways, I give you my address, my phone number. You be in touch sometime.

God Bless,

Alphonse

Jo,

Un mot pour te dire à bientôt, sinon aurevoir. I am leaving for the country as I told you I would. The time has come. I will be going alone it seems. It was this way: I was sitting beneath the orange tree in Tonton Léo's back yard. The scent of the blossoms made me heady as they fell softly to the ground in clumps like manna from the sky. The two of them came in Tonton Léo's new Ford Wrangler Jeep, red with black trim, imported from Miami only days ago. I did not think I had to make my presence known. I thought they would fight about politics and Charles would come to find me. But their voices did not clash. It was no secret that Tonton Léo wanted Charles to fill the empty space for the sons he never had. And Charles was nodding, acquiescing, taking money from Tonton Léo's hands and following him into the house for a glass of rum and Coke on ice. How I hated them both when I realized that I had been a spy for the wrong side. How used and soiled I felt when I remembered making love to Charles with every atom in my body screaming to become more than myself for him, only him. Ah, you see, this is how eyes are opened. You wake one day out of a deep slumber to look around you and see you stand alone.

It has been easy to sit in this yard and wish for revolution. Of course, revolution will never happen if people like me sit on our bottoms and look with pity on the women and men we enslave on behalf of a corrupt, corrupt economy which passes for capitalism! And so I must go, leave this behind. I send you something to remember me by. I will need nothing except my faith in St. Marie. Ezili, *bien sur*! You, too, I am sure, carry her in your heart. Carry me there with her, if you can.

  Bises,

   D.

A solid gold medallion falls out of the envelope. I hold it up to the light and read the tiny engraved words spreading like a halo around the figure of Mary, rays shooting out from her hands, standing on a stone and rising like the Goddess of Love emerging from the sea to reach the shore of ancient Kypris: "O Mary Conceived Without Sin, Pray For Us Who Have Recourse To Thee." I think of Désirée, her younger face struggling to close out the suffering of others when she was a child. And now she was off to save our people. I could think only of my small hand resting in hers when we walked the streets in Port-au-Prince around Tonton Léo's house in search of playmates. I could think only of how I had wanted to be just like her, how lucky I'd thought I was to be the one to hold her hand in this way, to have someone to trust so wholly. And I wondered if that luck would hold, or if, being Haitian, luck wasn't just an unsolvable puzzle you were born with. We look into the face of the world like bastard children waiting forever to be embraced. We stare blankly into the dark, as if someday a new sun will rise and penetrate the deepest reaches of the land, as if someday there'll be a cure for the pestilence gnawing at the bones of both old and young: the hunger for recognition. I feel the weight of the medallion in the palm of my hand and see my life becoming bitter as the leaves of the yew.

CHAPTER TWO

When I close my eyes, I dream of Désirée and I as children. I dream of her laughter, gurgling like the waters of a fall sinking into a pond at the bottom of a cave. I see her, arms outstretched, as she runs through my grandmother's yard like a bird in flight. In my dream, she is silhouetted against the sky, coming towards me. Laughter rises from my throat to meet hers. She takes my hand and our arms join together like hydroplanes at an air display I had seen on cable TV, coming from Grand Forks, North Dakota into our Winnipeg living room in the summer of '78. It is still that summer and I am miles from Canada and flying through the air with my best friend in the world, and my skin has lost its Canadian pallor to match hers, a sienna brown.

We run through gusts of wind as if nothing in the world could stop us. Grandmother sits on the cement stoop at the back of the house and taps her heels on the rose-coloured bricks of the courtyard floor. It is Sunday morning and we are still in our Sunday best: frilly sundresses with lace patterns on the bodice, shiny leather shoes with invisible heels and gold buckles on the sides, and bows in our hair matching our socks (green for me, yellow for Désirée). Dust is flying everywhere. It doesn't matter, because we are in our private heaven, just the three of us, and nobody can tell us what to do.

Later, Désirée and I are lying on the bed in the guest room in our underwear, having taken off our dresses and hung them in a wardrobe which is older than both of us put together. It is even older than our ever absent mothers, passed down through the generations, but stopping with Grandmother because there had been a glitch somewhere along the line about the significance of preserving the past. Something about moving forward and progress being about letting go rather than holding on. Something my mother tells me as she holds my hand when the plane lurches towards the landing strip at the Port-au-Prince airport and the engines screech and make our ears pop – twice.

Désirée and I look up at the ceiling, its whiteness fissured by black cracks in the paint.

"Do you ever wonder why things get old like that?" Désirée asks me. "Nothing ever stays the same, does it?"

"I guess not," I say, just to say something. I don't know what she is talking about, except that she looks different since the last time I saw her. She has bumps on her chest where I am just flat like Alphonse, and she does not take her undershirt off any more to swim in the pool at Tonton Léo's house in Kenscoff as she used to. She is fourteen years old now. Almost grown, my Grandmother says. She even talks about boys now, the ones she would never kiss and the ones she dreams about kissing. Sometimes she talks about girls like that too, which ones are pretty and whether or not they think she's pretty. I miss the old Désirée who didn't care a fig about what other people thought, except for me and Grandmother and Alphonse, and would tell them so. And then she talks about the big old stinking world and all the *châteaux* she plans to see when her father comes to take her back to France with him forever. She gets up from the bed and takes out a bag filled with objects he has sent her from a place called Grenoble. Sounds like *grenouille* to me, like a frog.

"See how much he loves me," Désirée says, "Here is the latest *parfum* from Paris, and look, I saved this for you." She holds something that looks like a chocolate bar, but when she opens up the paper the stuff is smooth and white with nuts stuck in it. "This is *nougat*," she says. "It's really great."

I nod as I chew on the stuff. It gets stuck in my teeth and I wonder if I will ever be able to speak again, or if it will give me a stomachache, which I don't want to have because Sunday dinner is always the best and biggest meal of the week. Désirée folds the paper back over the candy and I am grateful to see her put it away for safekeeping. "We can have more later," she says, as if it is a golden treasure. "Now I want you to tell me everything there is to know about Canada. Is it really cold? Are there really mosquitoes that eat you up and make you sick for weeks on end?"

The nougat sticks in my throat and I think I might choke to death. This is the first time Désirée has ever asked me about my life out there and I don't want to tell her anything. Because, if I do, it will mean that I am no longer just visiting abroad. It will mean that I am visiting her and Grandmother and I have become one of those distant relatives we use to laugh about when they came over to Tonton Léo's. The men would chomp on their foreign cigars and show off their new gold watches. The women tugged at wisps of freshly cut hair and demonstrated the elasticity of the soles of the shoes they had bought for work in offices where they didn't have to get coffee for the boss and air conditioning was on all the time. I thought that if that was what happened to you once your age reached two digits, I would forego birthday presents and stay eight forever.

So, I don't tell her about having to take the bus to school huddled against Sara in the long back seat where you feel everybody is staring at you because they can and you have nowhere to hide. And I don't tell her about the lady down the street who looks a lot like Grandmother simply because they are both grandmothers, except that this woman's hair is white and her teeth are straight and her skin gleams like the flesh of fresh salmon caught from the stream. They found her frozen to the floor of her bedroom in the winter. I still don't understand how no one missed her for all of those days and not known that something was terribly wrong. I noticed that she hadn't waved to me from her window with her calico cat sitting on her lap for one long week. The cat would cock its head at me and meow from behind the glass pane, sitting alone on the window ledge, and I would assume that the woman was out shopping or one of her daughters was there fixing her a cup of tea and a plate of shortbread cookies – which she liked a lot because that's what old English ladies like in the afternoon before they sit down to watch *Coronation Street* on the TV. I know, because she had me over twice and that is what we did. Now she is gone and I didn't get to say goodbye. So I show

Désirée the scars from my mosquito bites instead and she "oos" and "ahs" like the old Désirée and says: "Cool" as she fingers the darker patches around my ankles and gasps, "Those mosquitoes must be huge!"

We hear the sound of metal being sharpened against stone out in the yard. Désirée leaps up from the bed, "Quick," she says, "You have to see this."

Grandmother's axe is embedded in the wooden stump next to the oven. The stump is full of crisscrossing markings from the axe blade. It looks as if it has rusted from rain, but there is hardly a cloud in the sky here, ever. Grandmother is rushing around in the far corner of the yard by the hen house, clucking after a chicken which keeps running away from her outstretched hands. After they dance around each other a few more times, the chicken finally squawks defeat and Grandmother holds its wings back together as if she is holding the claws of a crab. I sit by Désirée on the stoop and hold my knees up to my chest as I realize that the stump isn't there just to split wood for the fire. Grandmother holds the bird down on the stump. It hardly moves. With her other hand she looses the axe, brings it up and back down in one smooth gesture into the fluffy neck of the chicken. The little body jerks and comes alive while the neck, bulging eyes and open beak lie still against the rusty wood. Grandmother lets go of the chicken's body and it leaps off to the ground and runs in circles, headless, as if to make a final protest.

"Isn't that incredible?" Désirée says, shaking her head. "It doesn't realize it's dead at all."

I go inside before I have to watch the feathered body jerk to a stop and collapse like people do in the movies when they have been shot. I sit at the kitchen table until Grandmother comes in holding the chicken by its feet and has Désirée help her pluck the feathers clean from the layer of fat she leaves on for me because I like to sink my teeth into the roasted, crispy skin before eating the meat itself. But I had never before connected the chickens behind the wire mesh with the wings and drumsticks on my plate. Grandmother watches me as she works and says, "*C'est comme ça la vie.* It lives so *we* may live."

At dinner, I make a silent prayer during grace so that God will not punish us. I concentrate on the taste of the red kidney-bean sauce each time I take a bite of the chicken and fight back tears, repeating to myself: It died so you can live, so *you* can live.

But that night I cannot stop the tears from streaming down my face when Désirée stands by the bed in her nightshirt and says, "I have a surprise for you." She opens up her left fist and cradled in her palm are the bones of the neck, stripped clean of sinew and cartilage, looking like carved pieces of driftwood. Désirée opens up her right hand and reveals a little rubber ball with multicoloured stars suspended in the golden plastic. "See," she says, "now you have your own set of Haitian-style jacks to take back to Canada with you. I made them just for you."

I push her hands way and roll up against my pillow.

Désirée sighs. "It's not so bad, you know. It doesn't really feel anything." I can feel her eyes on my back, but I pretend to be falling asleep. I hear the bones falling against each other as she puts them in the sock drawer, which always makes an odd clicking sound when it closes. I feel the mattress yield against her weight and I wish we could go back to the morning. And I wish I did not know where chicken legs came from. And I wish I did not know that my Grandmother's hands could kill as easily as they could hug you when you least expected it.

★ ★ ★ ★

C - E - R - C - U - E - I - L. I like to write down the letters over and over again. Then I spell the word in lower case letters: c - e -r - c - u - e - i - l. Then I spell it in cursive writing which is not something I do well, but I can pretend it looks as good as my mother's handwriting on her grocery list: *cercueil.* I imagine the horrified look that would appear on my mother's face if she read the list I have composed for today's English lesson. We had to bring in three words to translate. Mine are: *cercueil, deuil,* and *âme.* Mme. Fréchette looks over my words at the beginning of class and checks them off without giving me so much as a nod for effort and goes on to the next person whose words are: *arc-en-ciel, chat,* and *pamplemousse.* "Those are nice words," she says to Marc, the boy who runs after me at recess to try and kiss me while his best friend, Pierre, runs after Sara.

I go to my seat and show my check marks to Sara who is busy trying to come up with her words because she doesn't believe in doing homework at home and makes things up from class to class, still managing to pull in respectable "Bs" and the occasional "A". I watch as Sara goes to the end of the line and writes out the words ten times as Mme. Fréchette has asked us to on the lined paper she hands out at the beginning of the class. We wait until she has finished checking everyone's homework before she tells us to try our translations and I stare at my words until they become blurs of squiggly lines.

Sara takes the sheet from my desk and writes out: coffin, mourning, soul. She gives me back the paper and translates her own words which she won't show me because she says they're dumb while mine are deep in some weird way.

I look at the words she has written out for me and I say them in my mind: *Cough-fin. Mor-ning. Sôle* – the last word like the dinner my mother fixes on Friday nights because Catholics like us can only have fish on that day. *Filet de sôle.* You have to be careful to roll each bite of fish around in your mouth before you swallow, to pull out the slivers of bones. It takes a long time to eat.

We get to draw pictures next. I draw a picture of a church and I am in the coffin at the front and my soul is an angel flying up to the steeple. I draw the angel as a blob with wings to show that I have become invisible and can go through the stained-glass window with the picture of Joseph holding baby Jesus in his arms, a baby lamb at their feet. Sara draws a picture of herself in her back yard, with a flower growing from a purple pot in midair, waving at her mother who is inside feeding the dog. So I know her words are: *jardin, mère*, and *Jo-Jo* (that's her dog). Mme. Fréchette has drawn a huge, red x by Jo-Jo. Sara has crossed out his name and written *chien*/dog instead, which shows that sometimes doing your homework has its good sides, except we both get the same grade, "Bs," and upside-down smily faces at the top right corners of our papers.

★ ★ ★ ★

We are still under the covers when Tonton Léo drives up in front of the house in his American gold and green jeep with the removable top. He is all smiles and hugs us all. *"Jou'né la bel,"* he says, taking in a deep breath and slapping his chest with his palms. He is wearing shorts and a T-shirt that says Coca-Cola across the front in block, red letters. "Get your swimsuits, girls." We have come out to stare at him from the doorway. "I'm taking you to a pool party." He turns to Grandmother and they start speaking in créole.

Désirée hands me a sock. "I put the ball and jacks in it," she says.

I finger the oddly shaped pieces in the toes of the sock and feel a tremor go up my spine. Silently, I tuck the sock into my overnight bag and forget about it as I wonder about the pool party and who might be gathered there in their garish suits sipping their drinks around the white tables. These would be arranged strategically around the edges of the water so that the conversations could flow noisily into each other.

In the car, Tonton Léo ignores us and sings "Choukoun" to himself until we reach the store where we buy things for the barbecue. It's the store for people who have money like Tonton Léo. You can tell this because the fruit isn't left out in the open air and everything is translated into English for the Americans who have houses in the area. Tonton Léo disappears into the store, leaving the noise of chiming steel bells hanging in the air behind him. We sit in the car and watch the people in the street, mostly children asking for change from everyone who leaves the store loaded down with their overflowing sawdust-coloured paper sacks.

"That little girl hasn't had anything to eat for a long time," Désirée finally says. Then, she calls out to the girl whose stomach balloons out from underneath a flowered print dress: *"Ou vlé mangé, pitit?"* Désirée is speaking to her as if she is a grown-up. She tells me to stay in the car and is swallowed up in the cluster of people at a sugar cane stall a few metres away. She comes back with three pieces of sugar cane and gives me one before finding the little girl. She is following an American couple back to their jeep half way up the street. The woman, wearing a straw hat and a loose cotton dress with a thin veil covering her freckled shoulders, is looking back as if she thinks a monster is about to swallow her. Back in the car, she locks her door and stares down at the little girl's empty hands clutching at the air outside the window.

Désirée takes the child's hand and the Americans speed away in a cloud of swirling dust. By the side of the road, they eat the sugar cane together. I look down at my own piece which is beginning to dry around the edges. During my time away, I have forgotten how to eat cane. A hand reaches into the car and takes the cane from me. Eric's hand and his voice, both soft like velvet, draw me out of the car: "I'll show you how it's done."

We walk to the back of the convenience store where the ground is damp with rotting pieces of produce left out for wandering strays, not necessarily animals. I almost slip on a soft avocado but Eric's hand steadies me. His hand is as large as my entire forearm. At eighteen, Eric's chest has grown into a barrel shape and muscles bulge in his arms and lower legs. He works in the fields most of the time but some days he finds work in the stores along this road. These have been flourishing as more foreigners come to claim the land they tell us is not good enough for planting. Somehow, the land always turns out to be good enough for estates with pools and stables and separate quarters for the people who used to think they owned the land and didn't need the papers to prove it. Eric makes funny faces to make me laugh as he shows me how to bite off pieces of the cane and chew them until all the sweet juices flow out and burst against your cheeks and dribble down your chin. We take turns until it is all gone. Eric wipes his face on the untucked tail of his shirt which is already grimy from the day's work. He reaches down to wipe my face for me and I laugh into the fabric until I notice that his hand is not moving away but keeping me from breathing.

I struggle against his hand but he uses it to cover my entire face. I fall to the ground pinned under the largeness of his body and feel his other hand grappling with my zipper until his fingers slide into the secret passage my mother has told me is made for making babies when I am older and married to someone who loves me. Eric is grunting above me and his fingers claw into me like a crab. When he finishes down there, his fingers glide up underneath my T-shirt – which has the Chiquita-Banana lady on it – and touch the places which have not grown out yet, even though I pray to the

Virgin Mary every night about them and nothing happens. I am in so much pain I feel like I am dying. Where is Désirée and when will it ever end and can I go to heaven now? I see the chicken hopping up and down and Grandmother's hands placing the table settings on the table Tonton Léo brought down from the capital just for her to put in her kitchen. I ask the Virgin Mary to take the pain away but she doesn't hear me. Instead, Eric rises to his feet and jerks me up with him.

He becomes all kindness and his hands shake as he straightens out my clothes and brushes off pieces of rotten fruit from the seat of my shorts. "Everything is all right," he murmurs. "See, you're all right. *Tout va bien, Bien.*" And I think that maybe this was all a dream the way he smiles at me, but Eric has never smiled at me like this, as if I have fallen off my bike and he is my kind older brother helping me out. I don't have a brother. And there is a shooting pain between my legs I have never felt before which goes right up into my brain and stays in both places at once, hammering against my bones.

It isn't a dream. I know it the moment we walk around the corner of the store and Eric stops when he sees Tonton Léo open his pouch of tobacco to fill his pipe. He grips me by the arm and points across the alley where a man is putting together a coffin in a dark shop. "If you say anything," he hisses into my ear, "I'll put you in one of those and bury you alive. *Tu comprends?*"

I nod my understanding and break loose from him to run back to my seat in the jeep, to begin to forget. Tonton Léo looks at me, at Eric. Says: "The two of you are old enough to keep yourselves clean. You look like a couple of pigs." He reaches over to smack my head playfully with his open hand. I cringe. "Oh, well," he smiles, "Kids will be kids." He slaps Eric on the back, who suddenly looks innocent, as if sweet potatoes would melt like butter in his mouth.

Désirée is back and she talks all the way to the summer house about the little girl in the street and the dangers she faces and what we must do for her. I am quiet in the back seat and try to think of something to say but there is something lodged in my throat, keeping me from speaking.

Later, I sit by the pool in my swimsuit and hold a cold can of banana flavoured Kola against my stomach. I am hoping the coolness will take away the burning there but all it does is make it seem sharper and unending. I keep an eye on Désirée as Eric tries to talk her into drinking some rum by the changing rooms. She only laughs and walks away. I know now why she is always talking about *who* she should be kissing.

★ ★ ★ ★

They call the game hide and kiss. I am running as hard as I can in the playground at the back of the school where tether balls are being smacked by kids too short to keep the ball from winding around the head of the pole. My sneakers slap against the black concrete. Marc runs behind me, yelling: "I'm going to get you." Laughter. We do this as soon as we are shepherded out of the glass doors into the fresh air for recess. We are in the fourth grade. I am running and running because this is what you must do to escape a kiss, but the object of the game is for the boys to tackle us on the grass at the front of the school, where no one will be looking, or to corner us behind the blue metal garbage cans and press their bodies against us. All for kisses we are not supposed to give freely.

I run and run and I run. I wish my mother would buy me the Adidas running shoes I keep asking for. Instead, I wear those canvas sneakers that went out with the first grade and twist your ankles around sharp corners.

Marc is breathing hard behind me and the fact that I can hear him means I am not running fast enough. He tackles me on the front lawn and laughs: "I've got you, Josèphe. I finally caught you!" And he crawls up against my body like a wrestler and gasps in my face. His black hair is damp and stuck to his forehead. The sun is at his back and I cannot see his face. All I feel is the weight of him like Eric's that summer and I know I am going to die. Again. I slap him over and over and over and he grasps my arms and holds them over my head. The grass is cool and damp against my skin. "What are you doing?" he asks. "All I want is to kiss you." Marc kisses me and rolls off. I am left staring at the sky and a cloud in the shape of a leaping sheep. Then the bell rings. Recess is over.

★ ★ ★ ★

"You would tell me anything, wouldn't you?" Désirée says this as a statement, letting go of the question as if there is no reason to ask it. We are back in our room in Tonton Léo's house. All the grown-ups are a little drunk from the pool-party. Bella is making steaming cups of coffee in the kitchen and serving them outside before the guests climb back in their cars to head for home, scattering any street vendors foolish enough to get in their way. Our mothers are whispering in the next room like little girls. They swam together in the pool, ignoring us as they went back and forth together and stopped in the middle to talk.

"Eric and I did it in the changing house," she whispers. "We did *it*."

I start crying and she shushes me. "You don't want them to come in here, do you?"

But I can't stop. Not now, not ever. I know what she has done and somehow "it" is different from what has happened to me and I know I will never be able to tell her.

"Why are you crying? When it happens to you, you can tell me all about it."

★ ★ ★ ★

"Did he kiss you?" Sara asks as she takes off the scarf her mother knitted for her all last winter. The scarf is a baby blue and white. "Pierre tried to kiss me, but I didn't let him."

"So," she stares at me, "did it happen?"

"Yes."

"How was it?"

"You know. Like a kiss."

"Was it a kiss kiss? Or was it like a peck?"

"A kiss."

"Well, you don't seem very excited about it. This means you have a boyfriend."

I don't tell her I must have two boyfriends since Eric is the first. I smile and walk to my seat.

I have decided to become a nun. They don't have to kiss

anything except the feet of the plaster statues stuck in holes in the wall at Church. I've seen them do it: they bend down and kiss the toes peeking out from beneath the sacred vestments of a Mary, a Joseph or a Jesus, and then they wipe the feet with a red towel and pass this on to the next woman behind them.

I sit at my desk and say five Hail Marys, which should do the trick, to wipe the sin of what has happened between me and Marc. The priest usually only gives me one Hail Mary to do after I confess after Sunday mass about forgetting to put my toys away or forgetting to pray for the hungry children back in Haiti. Five should do it. But it will take a lifetime to wipe Eric away. A lifetime of sacrifice and devotion.

★ ★ ★ ★

A week after the pool party, Tonton Léo takes us to the sea instead of to Grandmother's house. He makes us wear old sandals in case there are poisoned fish shaped like stones at the bottom of the water. What he doesn't seem to know is that if you walk far enough away from the shore, your feet can't touch the bottom and you are safe.

I walk away from everyone to greet the sea and swim as far out as I can. In the ocean, I am not afraid. For a moment, I have escaped them all. I stretch out my arms and legs and all there is is more and more water surrounding me, holding me up, keeping other bodies from falling on me like storm clouds. I lie back with my face to the heavens and close my eyes. Then, I hear Désirée call me back.

When I walk out of the sea to meet her voice, I take off my sandals. The black sand feels hot as molten steel beneath my feet. For a long time, all I feel is pain and wonder why I put myself on solid ground, a disruption between the meeting of sea and sky, the endless stretch of blue hope whispering to me from behind.

CHAPTER THREE

Loss follows me through life like a second shadow. "Me and my shadow" was one of the songs they taught me in preschool in Canada. It was supposed to be cute and light-hearted, fun. I remember wanting only to disappear, become a shadow myself.

"*Répêtez. Repeat. Tous ensemble.*"

"One. Two. Three. . . "

"*Allez-y.*"

Where are we going?

They did not understand why I refused to sing. They did not understand that I thought it was a betrayal.

"*Josèphe, il faut que tu participes!*"

Participate? In my own destruction?

I would sing *Ti Z'oiseau* in my mind as we sat around the low preschool table. It was almost fall and still I was resisting, sensing that I was being told to become someone other than who I knew myself to be.

The heat, the sweat, all the discomforts of that Canadian prairie summer come back to me in waves of nausea. I would lift my thighs one at a time from my chair to air them. Sticky with sweat, they held me captive in my vinyl blue seat like suction cups. How unfree I felt: a tiny person sitting in a tiny chair at a tiny table.

The letters of the alphabet (**a** "apple/ail", **b** "boy/bébé") wrapped themselves around the classroom on a scroll on the wall halfway between floor and ceiling. The walls were painted a deep, aquamarine blue which made it easier for me to dream, to pretend that I was home with Grandmother and Désirée, going to market for a bagful of ripe plantain and fresh string beans. In her back yard, Grandmother would sit us down on either side of the wooden table, bleached white by the tropical sun, and set the beans between us in a mahogany bowl. And as she expertly plucked the chicken she would roast for our supper, we would proudly pull the strings from the ends of the pods and split them open with our thumbs, pushing the small beans out into an untidy pile. Désirée and I would giggle until grandmother chided us for taking our time with such an important task.

My daydreams made language class bearable.

"Jo, tu ne prononces pas tes 't-h'."

Stick my tongue between my teeth to make that sound? I was revolted at the thought. I had already been taught to hide the whites of my teeth when I smiled, to close my mouth when I ate. How could I stick my tongue out to make a sound I could barely hear? It was simply too much to ask. Obscene.

"Répêtons ensemble : Tee**th**. **Th**e. **Th**rough."

All together. Teef. Ve. True. I did not realize that these sounds mattered.

Our teacher, Madame Fréchette, would take me aside at the end of each day and tell me that I would never amount to much, never become a true Canadian, if I did not make a more concerted effort to blend in. It's the end of the summer, she would say, and still you resist.

That summer was endless. *Interminable. Infernal.* As in: *Cessez ce bruit infernal mes enfants.* Désirée and I look up to see Grandmother frowning, her chestnut brown hands white with chicken feathers. We would laugh, choking on tears turned to hiccups. Madame Fréchette did not understand that it was a betrayal. **Betray:** *be disloyal to, assist the enemy of; give up (person etc. to enemy); reveal treacherously; reveal involuntarily; lead astray; betrayal n.*

Before preschool, before the language classes, the summers were ours. Mine and Désirée's. When I was four and Désirée a worldly ten years old, I thought she knew everything, much to the annoyance of my parents who, try as they might, could not keep us apart.

My parents and I left Canada behind that June of '74 in a haze of thick clouds. Hours later we were circling the landing strip off

49

the coast of Haïti. It was amazing to me to think that Grand-mother and Désirée lived here all year long and could walk the sienna-brown roads of the mountains without having to worry about their vacation drawing to an end, of having to leave all of the comforts of home behind. But these were fleeting thoughts. Butterflies filled my stomach as the plane began its descent towards the green-blue sea which would await me with open arms every Sunday afternoon for the next four weeks.

On the ground, we were quickly hustled past the long line of tourists by an aunt who worked for the airline. Our bags were opened. I watched as a man dressed in khaki turned over my clothes and pawed through my underwear, all the while fixing me with an unpleasant stare. He laughed as he uncovered my teddy bear. I had carefully hidden him in a crevice between comic books and light cotton shirts. "*Ou pa Ayisyen,*" he said. "*Ou étranjé pitit. Sé étranjé ou yé vrè.*"

A stranger! How could I be a stranger? I pointed to Grand-mother as she patiently awaited us behind the red line separating the customs area from the arriving masses. The guard laughed again. "*Sa pa fè anyen.*"

She means nothing, he was saying.

Confused, I followed my parents.

The huge embrace Grandmother greeted me with made the discomfort of the encounter with the guard melt away. It was as if all our time apart had been a dream. I breathed in her scent of herbs and spices and the delicate perfume which made me think of dried rose petals crushed to powder. Every gift she had sent to find me in Canada had had that wonderful, comforting fragrance trapped in the folds of the pink Kleenexes she used for wrapping paper.

Soon, I was wriggling out of her arms to find Désirée's hand. We had so much catching up to do. We chattered ceaselessly in the car. Tickled at the prospect of being away from their restrictions and of having Grandmother to ourselves for days, we quickly kissed our parents goodbye. First, we had to drop them off at Tonton Léo's, a house now heavily guarded with chained, barking German shepherd dogs. Then we were off to my grandmother's home where we were going to be left for the week as our parents took stock of their lives, free (they said) of our petty demands.

At Grandmother's, Désirée and I reclaimed our relationship. We had developed a short-hand way of communicating which was often wordless. This we had learned from Grandmother who whistled and sang as she worked about the house, but rarely spoke – to us or to herself. From her, we learned that we could convey more with the gesture of a hand, a facial expression, the way we carried ourselves, or touched.

"Do you remember all this?" Grandmother asked as she laid my suitcase at the foot of a double-bed. "I have something special planned for us this afternoon."

Désirée and I pretended we did not know what the surprise was and clapped our hands with joy. "What is it? What is it?" we cried, as if our grandmother had never planned special things for us to do every time we were together.

"Get your smocks on."

We followed her out to the kitchen as we tied each other's smocks behind our backs. On the kitchen, table bowls of every size were arranged in an orderly half circle. She had placed in them flour, salt, pepper, iced water, and the secret, flavourful ingredients which, unmeasured, made *paille*, the light fluffy fritters she sometimes had Janine take down to market to exchange for fresh eggs.

"You sit here," Grandmother said, as she waved me into the smallest chair at the table, "and hand the bowls to Désirée as I tell you."

These were our cooking lessons. Another language with its own syntax. Désirée stood by me, all smiles, and took the ingredients from me, measuring each of them with what was becoming an expert hand at such a young age.

"Let's play a game," she said, "Jo, you choose."

"I want to play Simon says."

Désirée rolled her eyes. Grandmother laughed, but still they indulged me.

"I'm starting," I said. "Simon says: eat some batter."

It was bitter from leavening powder and they grimaced at the globs on their fingers.

"Simon says: touch your nose."

They left flour marks on the tips of their noses.

"Kiss me!" And they did. On both cheeks. "You lose," I squealed. "I didn't say Simon says!"

Next came the frying of the dough. The lard from the pantry had been cut and already melted in a heavy pan. Grandmother had us stand well behind her in case the oil splattered. I had to crane my neck to see the miracle of the dropped batter swelling into golden puffs. After letting the fritters drain on a clean towel we would eat them with small lumps of goat's cheese for a midday snack. But that moment never came.

It was still early in the afternoon. A mangy, stray dog, attracted by the smell of the cooking oil, came running from the courtyard and into the kitchen, jumping up on Grandmother's back and pushing her towards the pan. Its contents splashed onto her. Grandmother screamed in pain: "*Amoé! Amoé!*"

We ran next door to Mlle. Dominique's house and banged hard on her screen door until we could see her walking slowly towards us from the cavernous darkness of the inner chambers of her home. We had heard many things about Mlle Dominique: that she had taken part in a foiled looting of the U.S. army base in the 20s; that she practised black magic on her back porch where late at night she could be heard speaking in an unnatural voice. We thought she spoke in tongues and that the white dresses she wore every Sunday, tied around her waist with a light blue sash, were evidence that she had joined a secret order. She was a *mambo*, a *vodou* priestess. As we ran to her house, all these stories had escaped our thoughts. We knew only that she was the closest person about and that grandmother was still screaming for help.

The screen door screeched open to reveal a small woman. Her face was creased like a riverbed at low tide, yet appeared ageless. She did not smile. "What do you want?" I hid behind Désirée, using her apron to protect me from the evil eye.

"It's Grandmother," Désirée said. "The oil spilled."

"I can see that."

We had not noticed that our own clothes had been spattered and stained by the flying oil. But it was Grandmother who was burning, not us. "It flew all over her tummy," I spluttered from my hiding place.

"*Seigneur!*" Mlle. Dominique moved faster than I had ever

thought possible. "Désirée, get the vinegar from the cupboard in the hall." She looked at me as if she had never seen me before. "You, stay out of the way. Carmel should know better than to have such smallfry as you in her skirts while she does serious things."

I tried to tell her about the dog coming from nowhere. She tut-tutted and pushed me aside. "Stay here."

I sat in Mlle Dominique's small living room among the bric-a-brac of a life that had spanned more years than I cared to think about. There were pictures of children like me on a side table at my elbow and I wondered where they had gone and why it seemed to me that I had no place anywhere.

Désirée and Mlle Dominique scurried about for towels, water and fresh dressings. Mademoiselle disappeared to the back of the house for a few minutes and came back with a blue jar of smelly salve she said would cure about anything.

"Don't worry," Désirée pulled at my braids, "I'll come back for you when it's all over."

I waited for what seemed an eternity on Mlle Dominique's lumpy green couch. Grimacing statues stared me down from every corner of the room. I was about to cry when the screen door swung open and a head peered through.

"*Josèphe. Sa ou'ap fè là?* Come, it's getting dark."

It was my mother. Her hand reached out for me and I clung to it.

"When the vinegar hit her skin it bubbled up into blisters," Désirée later reported. "Grandmother fainted when she saw and Mademoiselle said that was good because she could put on the salve without worrying about hurting her."

It was morning and I was crying when Désirée, at last, came to find me. No one had seen the dog and it was clear that they all thought it was my fault. Mlle. Dominique had told them as much. They thought I had invented the dog to hide my guilt and that I was crying at the relief of having been found out. Aside from Grandmother, only Désirée knew the truth, but she had kept quiet as she had been taught to do – to be quiet and to do as one is told.

"That's all that happened. She's sleeping now. Your mother went to stay with her."

"What about us?"

Désirée shrugged her shoulders. "We stay here with my parents and Tonton Léo."

"My ear-s are bur-ning." Tonton Léo came striding into the room.

I did not like him. He had an affected way of speaking, exaggerating every syllable of his words as if we were all too stupid or slow to understand what he was saying. He had been to all sorts of places, to Africa, to France, to South America, and he thought this gave him a special dispensation from sparing our feelings. He also hated Grandmother because she insisted on speaking to us in Créole. The speech of fools, he often said to my mother. If you don't want Josèphe to speak as if she has pebbles in her mouth, keep her away from Carmel. I heard him say this with my own two ears.

"Haven't you girls seen enough of each other?" He lifted Désirée from the bed. "You go down and see to breakfast with the women." Then he turned to me. "You and I must have a talk about yesterday."

He closed the door behind Désirée and stood at the foot of my bed. Tonton Léo was a large man and I had seen him beat Alphonse, the house boy, viciously, with just the open palms of his hands. I started to sniffle uncontrollably.

"Stop that. That does not work with me."

I bit my lower lip.

"I want to tell you that I have one rule in this house that no one is allowed to break. Not even my sister's child. I will not tolerate lies. Do you understand?"

Without looking up, I nodded.

"Lies are the devil's way of putting your soul at risk. But you don't want to be in the devil's clutches, do you, Josèphe?"

Again I nodded, thinking all the while that he was the devil with his long hands and pointy nails, the v-shaped sideburns that made his grin, so much like my mother's, seem menacing.

"You're lucky she's all right."

At those words, I looked up, stunned.

"That's right," Uncle Léo went on, scratching at one of his sideburns, "it could have been much worse. And then where would you be?"

I could just imagine: the burning flames of damnation. He had said it often enough. I tried to escape from Tonton Léo's slow, painful French in a daydream, and then vowed revenge, for myself, Désirée and Grandmother, on his torturing mind, but then a ruckus interrupted his long-winded speech. Bella, the house cook, was screaming. Her yells, muffled by the heavy door to my bedroom, rose from the living room where we both ran to see what was going on. Bella was running around the room, upsetting chairs and the expensive lamps I had been told never to turn off and on by myself. She held a broom above her head, every so often bringing it down with a lethal swoop. And every time she brought the broom back over her head, she swore loudly. My uncle bristled at her sacrilege as she invoked the saints and God and almighty Christ. There was some small animal in the room. I thought it was a lizard because you could hear the clicketing of its small paws against the linoleum of the floor.

"*Kisa?*" My uncle had slipped into his native tongue.

"*Sé rat*," Bella answered. "*Nou genyen rat nan kay.*"

"That's not possible. I told Alphonse to take care of those pests days ago. I gave him the poison myself."

Bella shrugged her shoulders and followed the little brown tail of the rat out the door to the stairwell which led down to the servants' quarters below the house.

"There it goes," she said. "It's his problem now. I'm done."

Bella put down her broom and gathered up her belongings. Without a further word she left the house with dinner half-cooked on the gas range. That was the last we saw of her for the rest of the week.

"*Tonnerre!*" Tonton Léo was beside himself with rage. He followed the rat's exit to find Alphonse.

Alphonse was ten and had lived in the house since the age of seven. He was Janine's son. At least, this was what Tonton Léo called him, rather than by his actual name. We had been told that he was taken in by Tonton Léo as a favour to Grandmother who had been close to Janine's mother in childhood. Janine's mother had made what Tonton Léo called "*un marriage de chien*", meaning that she had married below her class. And then, to make things worse, her husband had left her when she was only a few months pregnant with Alphonse. (He had left without a trace, leaving everyone to wonder why and where he had gone.) Janine had never regained the position that belonged by rights to graduates of the well-known Catholic school for girls, Saint Anne's, in the upper hills of Port-au-Prince.

At the top of the stairs I eavesdropped as Tonton Léo told Alphonse how disappointed he was in him, that he was a failure just as Janine had been. The rest of the speech was a slightly modified version of what he had been unable to complete in my room just before.

When I heard Tonton Léo's feet coming back up the stairs, I hid in the kitchen and waited until he entered his study and closed the door behind him. I knew he would be there for hours and emerge only at dinner with a glazed look in his bloodshot eyes, smelling faintly of rum and stale mints.

Désirée was already at the bottom of the stairs with Alphonse when I finally ventured out of my hiding place. They were crouching over something. I squeezed in between their legs, demanding they let me see what they were doing. Alphonse handed me a dried ear of corn. In front of them were three rats, brown in colour, and thinner than I expected. They looked no different from the animals my Canadian friend Sara kept in a cage in her room and called gerbils, except these seemed much better behaved.

Alphonse was feeding them dried pieces of corn with the tips of his fingers. Désirée was doing the same. I had only two choices: to run to find Tonton Léo and tell, or to remain quiet and watch. What if someone found us? Wasn't this a bad thing we were doing?

I was silent and handed the pieces of corn I pulled from the ear to Alphonse, who nodded at me and smiled. We were there crouching in the dirt for a long time until all the corn was gone. Then, Alphonse stood up and stamped his feet at the rats who ran to hide in the tall grass beyond the stones of the stoop. "*Sal rat*," he screamed three or four times, so loudly my ears hurt. Désirée also yelled "dirty rat" a few times, stomping her feet as she did so.

Tonton Léo came running from his study, breathless. "Did you get them, Alphonse? Did you get the suckers?"

"Of course," Alphonse said haughtily, "This is what I'm here for, isn't it?"

Tonton Léo ignored Alphonse's cheekiness and slapped his thighs in triumph. "At last. I hope the poison works." Then, an enquiring look came over his long face as he saw Désirée and myself standing behind Alphonse. "What are you girls doing in this part of the house?"

Désirée stepped forward. "We were helping. We," she grasped my hand, "we put some poison there, and there, and there." She pointed to the far edges of the stoop where the grass was growing through the loose soil between the white stone slabs.

"That's right," Alphonse chimed in, "they were helping."

Tonton Léo beckoned for me to come to him.

"Do you remember what I said this morning? No lies?"

I nodded.

"Were you helping Alphonse?"

I nodded yes and heard Alphonse breathe relief behind me.

Tonton Léo squeezed me hard on the shoulder. "O.K., the both of you, up the stairs. And don't let me catch you here again."

That night, I dreamed that Tonton Léo was coming to get me with a big broom swinging above his head, to take me to meet the devil. But just as I was about to confess, Alphonse and Désirée came to fetch me, followed by an army of brown gerbils. They took me by the hand and made me swear never to speak of our secret to anyone.

In my memory, that summer holds a secret magic. I am remembering it now because my grandmother has just passed away. A week ago today, Tonton Léo phoned to tell me. I hung up the phone on his voice when he began reminding me that her health had begun to fail that summer long ago when the pan of scalding grease had left her with a scarred, discoloured belly.

I think of Grandmother, of the last time I saw her, some four years after that fateful summer when everything was changing so quickly. Tonton Léo had kept Désirée and I away from her as much as possible and gotten us a French tutor. Everything was changing – the way we spoke, the way we played, the secrets we kept. On my last visit home, my grandmother's speech had been unintelligible to me. She had pulled out an old photo album on her verandah and tried to explain the pictures to me, but I had no way of translating her words. There seemed nothing left between us but the ghost of that stray dog that leapt up behind her for a taste of her cooking.

I walk around my cramped apartment wondering whether there was anything I could have done that summer that would have changed the course of our lives. My resistance had not lasted long. I was now fluent in French and English. I knew nothing of my grandmother's Créole, the language of fools.

I sit on my bed and find myself floating above that familiar terrain: the bald mountain ranges, the patches of brilliant colours checkering the valleys, the endless winding roads leading to Janine's market stall. When I walked those roads so long ago, I had thought that my feet were roots enough for belonging.

I fall back on the bed and cry over all that has been lost. I want to find Désirée. Only she would know how I feel. Only she could understand my loss of tongue, my need to smell Grandmother's pink Kleenexes stuffed in boxes marked fragile, and the emptiness I feel at her passing from this world, with nowhere to turn but inwards.

Slowly, Tonton Léo's words over the phone line come back to me. Désirée had disappeared just a few weeks before the funeral. They had seen her about town, but where she lived, no one seemed to know. She had made friends with the street kids, the ones nobody claimed to train as their personal house boys or girls. When her family saw her in the streets they would call out to her, but she would not acknowledge any of them. She was losing weight, the dimples in her cheeks had flattened out into long lines. Her skin was burnt darker. She had cut her hair and wore it in tight curls. All this, they thought, was evidence that she had turned her back on who she was, on who we were. All those years lounging in the shade at the beach – all for nothing. She had become ordinary, foolish.

"A fool girl," Tonton Léo had said. "Don't do as she does. Your grandmother may be dead but this is no time to lose your sense of right and wrong." All this he had said in his perfect imitation of a Parisian accent.

I pick up the picture of Alphonse, Désirée and I sitting on my grandmother's porch that last time. I was eight, Désirée and Alphonse, both fourteen. We were not smiling. We were so grown up. So knowing that we would not stand together like this again.

CHAPTER FOUR

I think grief must be the colour of tarnished silver. Silver tarnished with disuse – and the smell of the cleaning fluid and soft rags for polishing up its surfaces.

White light streams through half-closed blinds as I stand by the island in my kitchen before night falls and life quietens. I bring out the pieces of silverware grandmother sent me with a note saying that she'd had a premonition of her end.

There are the coffee spoons with carved swirling handles, the ice prongs with claws, the elegant table setting for four – all there, wrapped loosely in the familiar Kleenexes. But I forget to change my clothes, tie a cloth around my waist like Grandmother would have done. Her scent rises towards me and still I do not stop to think about where I am and where she is. Or, where we are not. I forget that I am in my apartment. That she could be anywhere.

I unfold the Kleenexes, spreading out the pieces on the counter. Methodically following the grain of the silver, I polish off the tarnish. And it is not my brown hands that I see, the colour of roasted almonds, but grandmother's, the colour of aged bark. Her long tapered fingers caressed the silver in just *this* way, turned each piece in *that* manner. My hands echo her hand's motions and I am lost in the swirl of the circles drawn by her palms against the cold metals, warming them like a lover.

As a child, when I watched her in her kitchen, I understood that such tasks made her who she was. It was her way of expressing hope for better things in life, though her hopes were always simple. The silver, not expensive gold or even the perfection of sterling, needed care, the touch of a hand to make it valuable, a treasure to pass on – even if incomplete. She had never had

60

enough money to buy the entire set and these pieces had long been in my possession, rotting away in the drawer. Perhaps if I had paid them more attention, I could have kept our bond alive and Grandmother would be here in the flesh, reminding me of the significance of small rituals in the life of a woman of the people.

I don't know how long I've been standing here, polishing the pieces, rinsing them under the tap, drying them with a soft, cotton towel before I realise the phone has been ringing, its shrill bell crying like an egret in the early hours of a Caribbean morning. I hear its cry a few more times before realizing that it is only the telephone. I finish polishing the last piece of silver and set it alongside the others. They shine like stones polished by the ebb and flow of sea tides. Pleased, I smile, and lift the receiver slowly from its hook on the wall.

"Hello?" The voice is Sara's, filled with anxiety and concern.

"Yes?"

"Are you O.K.? How's it going? Do you need anything?"

Sara. As long as I've known her she has talked this way, never separating one thought from the next. Since we met in first grade I have envied her facility with language, the ease with which she conveys her every thought and emotion.

"I was just doing some house work. Nothing special."

"Oh." There is a long pause. A hesitation. "Would you like some company?"

I am not sure what company means at this moment. "Sure," I say.

"I won't be long. Just give me some time to change and then I have to pick up some things on my way, you know, errands and such. Do you need anything?" She does not wait for a response. "Of course you need some soup and bread and pasta. You've been cooped up for too long. It's been three days. Maybe we could go for a walk?" Now she waits. I can see her dark eyes trying to pierce the distance bridged by the long cords of telephone wire, trying to guess my every need. "Well," she finally says, "I won't be long."

"O.K." I am surprised at how calm my voice is, as if nothing has happened. "O.K., O.K." Even cheerful: "I'll see you when you get here." And then I return the phone to its hook, oh so gently, and then I wait until I hear Sara's footsteps on the cement blocks leading to the front door of the building, as if nothing in the world could keep her away.

I wait for her to knock before opening the front door. Even now I don't want to seem too needy. I don't want her to imagine me waiting for her.

Her face awaits me patiently, peaches and cream complexion framed with dark, straight hair shaped with some difficulty into a bob around the base of her jawbones. A smile draws itself from the thin lines of her lips. She cocks her head to the right, assessing the situation, extends her arm out towards me. Dangling from her fingers is a half-open Safeway bag filled with lettuce, tomatoes, cucumbers, canned soups and teas. She must think I'm an invalid. I take the bag from her and step back to let her in.

She walks into the darkness, gasps: "When was the last time you opened a window in here? Where's the sunshine? You know, it's not just plants that die without light. People need it too." I watch her hurry from room to room parting curtains, prying windows open. I let her do what she feels she must and go back to the kitchen. I am almost afraid that the silverware will have vanished and need to reassure myself that it is still there, shining in the darkness. And it is. In no time at all, Sara is there, curious, wanting to help. She tugs open the blinds, peers over my back. At twenty, she still has the mannerisms of her child self. I see her eight years old, peering over my narrow shoulders to see if I am spelling my English words correctly, whispering to me when to change the letters from "their" to "there". I relied on her to make sense of the life around me, to filter the right from the wrong. "Oh," she says, spying the silver pieces, "How pretty. Where did those come from?"

"Grandmother. Aren't they nice?" I say, as if I am hosting a cocktail party. Then, without warning, I feel the need to tell her things about Grandmother so that someone else will understand why I cannot focus on anything except the past.

We sit in the living room, on the sofa Sara helped me to buy from the Salvation Army store downtown. It's a putrid green and yellow and the fabric is rough and uncomfortable – from the sixties. To hide its ugliness I have thrown a pale, multicoloured knitted shawl on it, tucking the extra fabric into the crevices. It's shabby but it works. I bring out the photo album marked "Haiti 1974-78" on the spine. The photo album is smooth to the touch, covered by a glossy paper that reminds me of the waxed sheets Grandmother used to wrap pieces of cane sugar fudge concocted for special events. I open the album so that its pages extend over both our laps and show Sara a picture of grandmother. "This is what she looked like when she was sixteen," I say.

"She looks so innocent," Sara whispers.

I finger the edges of the photograph which has slipped out from beneath the plastic cover of the page I have been shifting back and forth. She does look innocent, yet worldly at the same time. The picture has a jagged crack running through it where it has been folded in two, as if someone had sat on it by mistake at some family reunion long ago when photos were apt to be strewn about. The crack runs like a healed wound across the face and chest of a young woman who holds an arrangement of hibiscus in her clasped hands. She is smiling one of those smiles that only exist in the studios of belligerent photographers. She is smiling tightly. On the right hand side of the crack I can make out the gold chain and cross I have seen hanging around my mother's neck all of her life. The girl's smile on that half of the picture beams a false happiness, a static satisfaction. On the left-hand side of the crack, the bouquet transcends the two-dimensional parameters of black and white and I imagine the light pinks along the outer petals, brilliant *rouge* within, the polleny wonder of the sticky stamen. They look both dead and alive, the stems crisscrossing one another. They are no longer rising from the ground but suspended in air. Do they know they are dying? Grandmother, who never let the flowers at the front of her house be cut, unless for a funeral, told me that flowers were gifts from above, a promise of things to come. The girl's smile on that half of the picture is mysterious, hardly a smile: a thin line ending abruptly in a skin taut with youth, elastic and smooth, rising high into seemingly endless cheekbones whose ascent is interrupted only by wisps of curly hair. "Yes," I say, "She does look vulnerable."

You cannot see this in the picture but her hair is soft, like raw silk before it has been processed into cloth. Soft and tight at the same time, resistant to the pull of hairbrushes and wooden combs dipped in oil, intended to smooth, straighten, provide the illusion of a tamed wilderness. The hair is parted, precisely, from front to back. In the picture, you cannot see how thick the braids are. They reach halfway down her chest. One, held captive behind the flowers, is hidden by the cup formed by the petals of the tallest flowers in the cluster. The hair is like a serpent, coiled, ready to pounce from Eve's garden.

You cannot see much in the picture below the breast bone, which undoubtedly heaves irregularly from the woman's attempt, at the photographer's insistence, not to move. If the picture was longer, if you could move the lens a little lower, cutting off the grey space above the head which tells you nothing, then you would see what I see: those fingers, those hands that held newborn babies, painted the pictures she hid in the dilapidated store behind the house, split wood on the stump of a rotten tree, built fires in the stone oven, kneaded bread, and fluttered like wings to accompany the rhythm of a story. But there are no pictures of the woman she would become, the dreams hidden in the hands that no one sees because the photographer moved them lower (*lower now, lower, that's right*, he would have told her, *that's just right and don't move*) and out of sight because he thought they were too large, unfeminine, the hands of a labourer and not of a *débutante*. And yes, she is wearing the dress that all the girls wore that year to mark their coming of age: a white tunic to signify purity, flowers embroidered in half circles from the neck down to a slight gathering above the breasts, pleats running down to the belted waist.

I hear Sara suppressing a laugh. Her voice comes to me from far away: "She looks like us here," fingernail tapping against the plastic page, "when we went to Catholic school. God, it's the same everywhere, isn't it? Why can't they make religion a pleasant experience?" She goes on to the next page, not waiting for my explanation, which is just as well because I am no longer thinking about the pictures but about how things were, back then, when I would see Sara one last time before the summer vacation, kiss her pet gerbils goodbye and feed them lettuce through the openings in their cages, and head for that distant home that I could not call home. *Haiti chérie.*

★ ★ ★ ★

First, there would be the dawn piercing bright through the fogged glass blocks that take the place of windows. The blocks are at least half a foot in depth, keeping us away from the heat and the distilled smell of sea salt and kelp. Within this room, the dawn is colourless. I hear Alphonse scraping coconut husks in the front yard, two levels below. I imagine the soft fruit, opaque and white as prairie snows, as he spoons it out into wooden bowls to place on the breakfast table – the table at which he will never sit – covered with the gilded cloth Tatie Rosaline, Désirée's mother, had given my mother as a wedding gift. I lie very still in the twin-bed which is mine for two months of every year. It is 1976. I am six years old. And I realize that whether I am here or not, lying still or sitting downstairs on the stoop, all of this is mine. The pattern of our lives is premade and carved in the very echo of our names.

Names matter here. At least, they used to. A person's name was like a passport, letting you into the desired circles, keeping you out of others, revealing if you were from country or city, poverty or riches, (if you were related to so-and-so who took leisurely trips abroad to Miami or Paris without a worry in the world).

I do not give my name much thought as I descend the stairs to the kitchen. I say hello to Bella and sit down with greedy anticipation. Today I am disappointed with a bowl of Rice Krispies. How un-Haitian can you get. I want my porridge, my bowl of *acassan* (even though I refuse to eat these same things in Canada). As I fill my bowl, little red nuggets tumble out from the waxed paper bag along with the beige, powdery rice-kernels. I squint to see if these are a prize of some sort but make out the wiggling bodies of stunned ants as they scramble around looking for a place to hide. There are dozens and dozens. "*Gadé*," I say to Bella, pointing at the bowl, "Look! Look what's in my bowl!"

Bella comes, followed by my aunt, Tonton Léo's wife, who squeals with disgust. "Bella," she exclaims, "get the child something decent to eat."

Bella frowns, crosses her arms across her chest. "A few little ants aren't going to do her any harm," she says, "Besides, they're nutritious."

My aunt shouts a few choice words at Bella who ignores her and goes about her business until my aunt leaves the room to find Tonton Léo. Bella mutters: "That woman thinks she's talking to a child." She turns to me. I am still watching the ants, fascinated with their wild excavations in my food. I am trying to connect these ants with those I had seen the day before crawling up the handrail on the outside stairs leading down to the helpers' quarters where Alphonse lives alone in a small room with only a bed and a washstand. At first, I had thought I was looking at a huge, exotic insect, but when I looked more closely I saw four ants carrying a piece of burnt flat-bread as big as a quarter on their backs. The ants in my cereal do not seem to like work; they are not about to lift one of those Rice Krispies. They must be looking for a place to sleep, but Rice Krispies are full of holes, everybody knows that; that's why they crackle. This is what my six-year old mind is thinking as Bella takes away the bowl, muttering to herself, and I watch her with my head propped up on one arm, waiting for a replacement, which comes in the shape of a sour grapefruit I cannot eat.

Laughter wafts up to the kitchen from the courtyard. Désirée has come for me and she is laughing with Alphonse. I strain to hear what the joke is about. It could be anything: frying bugs with a piece of glass, chasing lizards into the distant grass, telling stories about the people of the house.

I leave the half-eaten grapefruit and hurry out of the house before Bella can discover that I have not finished my breakfast and summons me back. Outside, the day is clean and bright like fresh scrubbed sheets. Désirée and Alphonse are waiting impatiently at the bottom of the stairs.

"What took you so long?" asks Désirée.

"The Queen had things to do," Alphonse teases.

Teasing isn't something I understand very well. I eye Alphonse, trying to get at the meaning behind his words. Alphonse has the smoothest skin I've ever seen, and round, brown eyes with eyelashes so long they seem fake. His hair is cut close to his scalp so that it looks like a little plastic helmet of swirls. He is thin but muscular from years of having to run around satisfying the whims of adults who pretend that his employment has nullified the fact that he is still a child. A child myself, and younger, I see Alphonse as an older cousin who will always have power over me even though I have grown two whole inches since the last time I saw him. He jiggles some objects in his pockets and I know why they were laughing. They have been playing marbles against the outer wall of the house , making them ricochet back into the circle drawn in the dust.

"Let me see," I say to Alphonse, pointing to the hand hidden behind the khaki cloth of his trouser pocket.

Alphonse laughs. He cloaks his voice in a sinister tone and brings out two marbles. "These aren't just for play." He tucks one marble into the palm of his hand and rolls the other between his thumb and forefinger. "There's magic in these. That's why they're called cat's eyes. You have to be careful how you look into them because they could decide to pounce on you and scratch your eyes out." He pretends to throw the marble at me, but holds it back before unleashing it. I've only glimpsed the marble but I want to know its power: it's smaller than the usual marble with a yellow streak surrounding the blue eye veined with green flecks. "I'll let you have it," Alphonse says, "if you run to the crazy woman's house and come back with a flower from her garden."

Désirée laughs. "She'll never do it."

And of course, that is all it takes for me to go back into the house to get the little vinyl purse my mother gave me for when I go on errands. It has a little mermaid, with blond hair tied in two bunches on either side of her head and a long blue fish tail where legs would normally be, sewn onto the flap which closes and opens with a twist of a gold knob. Inside, there is a matching oval mirror with a plastic handle. The mermaid's head is on the back of the mirror, smiling, so you can pretend that she is you on one side and that there is someone else looking back at you from the silvered side of the mirror. I place the bag across my shoulders and I'm ready to face the crazy woman.

"I want to see the marble first," I say to Alphonse and Désirée, who are surprised to see me and have gone back to their game.

Alphonse pulls it out of his pocket. It is as lovely as I remembered it. It glitters in the sunlight and the eye is alive with flecks which are not only green but gold, and the yellow is lined with a thin purple line that it is so clear it seems white. I look up at Alphonse (I still have some inches to go before I reach his shoulders) and swallow the bitterness which has begun to form at the base of my throat. "All right," I say, "*Li ou Métrès Folie?*"

Alphonse laughs at my pitiful créole. "We will show you."

I walk behind them as we go in single file along the walls that protect the house from intruders. We have to be very quiet, avoid stepping on loose gravel or dry twigs fallen from the trees in the front yard. The walls are taller than any of us, even Alphonse. They are so tall they kiss the sky with the jagged mouths of broken bottles of all colours: brown, green, gold, purple and blue. I wonder why the sky does not bleed. The bottles were set in the wall when the concrete was still wet. They are there to tear open the flesh of anyone who dares to touch them. Looking up, I know why I want the marble so badly: I want to stop the bleeding: I want all the colours wrapped up neatly in a little globe so they cannot escape, so I can take it out of my pocket whenever I want and show it to Sara when I go back to school in Canada and tell her I have the power to stop death, to heal where only hate has been.

Alphonse and Désirée elbow each other in play, trying to make each other fall off balance into the deep ruts at the side of the crumbling asphalt. I tag along behind, the forgotten one. My skin feels as if it is being lifted off the flesh in the scorching heat. I have an urge to peel off my clothes and jump in the pool, but we are too far away from home. I lose them around a corner and wander a bit on my own until I see their bodies wavering like smoke signals at the fork in the road ahead. When I reach them they are sniggering and I can tell they're planning to do something to me, something to do with the crazy woman. The fence at the corner is low, made of wire-mesh, flaking white paint into the dust. The gate is swinging back and forth on a broken hinge.

Désirée smiles: "The crazy woman is in there. You must go into the yard and get one of the roses blooming by the verandah. See?" She points to the house, sheltered beneath trees turned bottle green with moss.

Alphonse brings out the marble and squints at it as if it is a precious stone he has just unearthed. "Just one rose," he says. "That's all it takes."

"But," I swallow, "There must be some mistake. This is Mlle. Dominique's house. She's not a crazy woman."

Désirée is smug in her reply, "That's what you think." She draws circles in the air with her right hand. "Bananas. Every once in a while she goes off. She's been this way ever since Delphi disappeared. Some people say it's she who did it with all her black magic ways and she just can't accept her wrongs."

Delphi. Disappeared? This is what happens when you're gone for too long. Names become ghosts and grown people become air. Delphi was Mlle. Dominique's son. He joined the U.S. marines when he was eighteen and sometimes he would send crates of Florida oranges or California dates back home, along with pictures of himself swabbing the deck or hoisting the American flag into the cloudy skies. Every summer there would be news like this: that person died, this one was murdered by the Macoutes, that one went into exile and those were sold to the Dominicans for cheap labour. It could make you lose a sense of the world around you.

"I'll do it," I say, my mind still set on winning the marble. I march into Mlle. Dominique's front yard hastily, so they cannot see the worry burrowing deep lines into my forehead. I clasp my purse to my side and walk gingerly through the tall grass, as if snakes are hiding there. Mlle. Dominique does not seem to be home. And I forget all about her as I approach the flower bed where the rose bush is growing wild from inattention. I look for the brightest red rose to pluck and find it hiding deep inside the overgrown branches locked together to form a nest of thorns. This is like looking at the Sacred Heart, I think, feeling overcome by the beauty. Knee-deep in catechism classes, I believed anything beautiful had come direct from heaven and think twice about removing the bud from its sanctuary. As I finally reach in, something falls on my right shoulder and keeps me from moving. At first, I think it is the hand of the Virgin Mother protecting the beauty she herself has made. But then I smell the unmistakable odour of old age – moth balls, stale urine and baby oil. It is Mlle. Dominique's hand, with its wrinkled skin and veins fighting to reach the air, which holds me.

"*Sa oua chèché pitit?*" she asks. Her voice floats to me through a

69

mist of cotton balls, every word falling heavy from her mouth. "*Sa ou vlé?*"

"*Rose la*," I say. "This one." I point to the rose.

"Ah," she says, "The hiding princess. Let me get it for you." Mlle. Dominique reaches into the thicket of thorns. Not one of the teeth sinks into the tired flesh as she nimbly plucks the flower from its base and brings it out, whole, into the sunlight. "*Voila*," she says and smiles. She is missing a tooth on the left side of her mouth.

"*Mè'ci.*" I take the flower from her and place it on the mirror in my bag. Mlle. Dominique looks at me from somewhere far away and I begin to grow afraid. She turns away from me and begins to search all around the rose bush and in the grass, as if she has just remembered something she has lost and needs to retrieve. "What is it? What are you looking for?"

Mlle. Dominique goes on searching, raking patches of soil with her chipped fingernails, and when she finally looks back at me there are tears flowing down her cheeks. "You see," she says, "I am looking for pieces of glass. There used to be glass from bottles everywhere on this soil before the house was built. It was everywhere I tell you. Delphi used to be afraid to walk barefoot in the yard. I used to laugh at him. But maybe he was right. I must have left some behind, somewhere. I must find them. This way he will come back to me and no longer be afraid. You aren't afraid, are you?" She does not wait for my answer, but goes back to lifting the soil in handfuls and letting it sift through her fingers.

"No," I say, "I am not afraid." I leave her there, crouching by the bed of roses.

Alphonse and Désirée are still waiting by the side of the road. Alphonse's fifteen year old cousin from down the road, Eric Laurier, has joined them and he wants to see the rose. I pull it out along with the mirror. I watch in horror as the mirror falls to the concrete, face down, and breaks into a thousand slivers. As I bend down towards the shards, Eric takes the flower and plucks away the petals, letting them glide on the air until they reach our shoes. In the glass fragments, my face is reflected in a thousand separate pieces. Alphonse picks up the mirror casing and grimaces, "*Sept ans de malheur!*" Désirée takes me by the hand and we start to walk back to Tonton's house. I turn back to Alphonse and ask for my marble, even though it seems meaningless now. He gives it to me without comment, and then I break away from Désirée to run the rest of the way home yelling, "She's not crazy! She's not crazy!" Mlle. Dominique was just a sad, grief-stricken woman.

I leave Désirée and Alphonse behind, this time knowing that they are the outsiders. And yet, I am not sure what it is that I have learned. It means, somehow, that I have come face to face with my ignorance. That I am ignorant, not blissfully like my Aunt and Tonton Léo, but ignorant as in lost, lacking insight, vision. I am the fruit of the coconut set on the wooden table to blanche in the sunlight. Désirée and Alphonse are the husks, thick with fibres like the roots of their knowing; they will remain as strong as I am weak. Or so they tell me, so that I will do anything they say, believe all their tall tales. It never occurs to me, until much later, that they are children like me, fumbling through a life they don't understand.

★ ★ ★ ★

"I don't remember seeing these before," Sara's voice calls me back down the tunnel of my thoughts to this too small living room cramped with books and unfinished term papers. Sara's fingers glide over a picture of me, aged eight, bopping up and down in the dark ocean, my face sombre with the effort to be still for a moment. I am captured in time like a piece of pineapple suspended in jello. But these are pictures I never serve up like dessert with coffee after an intimate dinner party. I store these away, as I do my memories, like precious metals, and after a time, I forget that they are there, aged, yellowing around the borders, keys to my dormant, lost life. Seeing them again seems to repair something which has come loose in my soul.

"You should show these to Georges," Sara says, "You really should. It would bring you two closer together. You know, I shouldn't be telling you this, but he told me last week that he feels you're keeping things from him. He worries about you."

Sara. Always trying to make things right because she does not yet know that events take place that change you forever and make life a blur of rights and wrongs running into each other like wet watercolours on paper. Georges is like her, always wanting to provide fixed answers where none are possible. The year we have spent together, he thought he was the answer to my silence.

The night of our first anniversary, a month ago, we sat in a chic revolving restaurant, where the only good thing on the menu was the sight of the city with its lights glistening like fireflies buzzing in a gloomy forest. The candlelight threw shadows across our gleaming white dinner plates. Georges' face seemed like a moon hovering in the distance. His green eyes were deep like craters. His voice stumbled as he told me he wanted our lives to be joined forever and my hands grew clammy with fright in his. He stopped speaking then but did not let go.

I know what he yearns for: to have a child with me, a miniature reflection of the love he believes we share. And all I can think of in return is the not wanting. I don't want to push some small being through my pain: to hear that small gush of wind as the rib cage expands for the first time to take in the air already polluted by the sweat and antiseptic of the delivery room. I don't want to give it that – a life already rushing towards death, when the first moment is the last in which everything is about her or him opening the tiny slits of eyelids to see a flash of light and nothing else for days on end. George does not know that what he wants is not mine to give. It has already been taken away.

I slipped my hands out of his and smiled promises I could not then imagine keeping.

I smile now at Sara in a distant, distracted way, and close the photo album to tell her it is time that she leave before the night turns into day. I need time to gather my thoughts one by one, like pieces of broken glass that need to be taken out of harm's way, to write it all down for myself, for Alphonse and Désirée, and for those who have brought us to this point. And all I can think about, as I sit alone in front of the typewriter keys encrusted with finger oils and dust, is the figure of Mlle. Dominique squatting in the dirt, like a hen, scratching at the earth for loose pieces of grain.

DELPHI
1956-1979

"All flesh is grass and all its beauty is like the flower
of the field."
Isaiah 40:6

It was not the time of the rainy season and yet rain fell in heavy cords of grey to meet the parched, burned soil of the mountains. There were no roots to meet the coursing waters, to hold on to the earth with sturdy, gnarled fingers, so the rivulets ran wildly through the crumbling dirt like blood bursting from the veins. Flowers bloomed and trees grew new leaves. The days were long and steaming hot.

A line of men dressed in white gabardine shirts and long, cuffed cotton pants zig-zagged through the wet underbrush, like ants building nests beneath the surface of the ground. Their heads were covered with wide-brimmed hats stiff with sweat. The leather of their work boots was cracked with caked mud. Their faces were long and pointed, bright beige like pumpkin seeds, fingernails browned from smoking the Camel cigarettes they had brought with them in waterproof cartons. They carried rifles in their hands, stiff like the stalks of fresh cane, and water bottles made of glistening metal on their hips. They listened, as they had been taught to do, for breaking twigs and the distant sound of the drums they had come to associate with the seamless mountains. Sometimes, they confused the rain with drums and each other's fearful steps with those of their enemies. Then they turned on each other in confusion, falling against the wet branches of almond trees like children learning their first steps.

On the other side of the mountain, in a clearing called Chabert in the Artibonite region of Haiti, a rectangular fence of steel with coils of barbed wire had been erected to surround green tents which crowded the ground like wild bushes. The rain pelted the triangular shapes into bowls of fabric that caught the water. The *cacos* stood in their stained and ripped clothing in a long line

74

stretching from one end of the wire fence to the other. They were looking towards the gate in the fence. With the rains would come the first fresh water in the camp, the first time that the scent of burgeoning plant life would reach them. Beyond the fence, men and women in long robes walked in single file down the unpaved road rutted by the wheels of so many army trucks.

The robed figures had walked on air, it seemed, so quietly had they come. A hand shot up towards the sky as they approached the *carrefour* at the front of the gateway to the camp, which was chained and locked. The group broke into a circle. Left of centre was a man with a long beard tied with a piece of string at its very bottom. The string dangled against his chest, sodden with water. His robes were white, like fresh goat's milk steaming in cool morning air. One by one, the followers stepped forward to hand the *houngan* offerings of chicks, palm oil or squares of cloth from tunics that had been worn at other ceremonies for *Fa, Papa Legba,* god of destiny. Each took a turn, made their offering and stepped back from the houngan as he took out a pouch tied against his chest to keep it dry from the rains. He brought out from the pouch the coarse cornmeal used to draw the circle of *Fa,* the endless cycle of birth, death, and second life. The face of the *houngan* moved spasmodically as sacred words fell from his lips like the whisper of the wind through the leaves of young palms. Each whisper ended with the rattling of his *ason.* The swaying bodies, listening with closed eyes to the pebbles and small bones of mountain snakes tumbling inside the shell of the *houngan's* ceremonial calabash rattle, replied softly by singing out the name of the departed spirit they wanted to keep among them: Chaaar-le-magne. This was the best they could do. They could not take the body and embalm it, first cleansing the skin with fresh spring water and then with a concoction of teas made from green oranges, lemon, mint, and *korosòl* leaves. They could not turn him over onto his chest, letting his saliva run into the pitted shell of a coconut, to protect his fluids from those who had betrayed him in the last hours of triumphant rebellion against the four year old invasion. They would not be able to whisper into his ears the thoughts he should keep as he journeyed ahead of them to *Ginen,* to the land of the ancestors.

This is the story told by my mother when she showed me a copy of a flyer concerning Charlemagne Péralte that the Americans had posted in all the public places in the cities, towns, villages shortly after his death, in November 1919. They called him DEFEATED. We called him THE CRUCIFIED ONE. Péralte, his eyes closed in a face with features so finely distinct that they seemed carved out of wood, was tied with a ship's cord to a door. He wore only shorts and these were ripped and mangled. Miraculously, his body showed no scars or cuts. He seemed so peaceful and yet so alive, as if he had not been conquered but was waiting to rise again.

Now it is my turn. I am Delphi Dominique, son of Mlle. Dominique, the woman who came out from the country, all the way to the hills of Port-au-Prince and built herself a life without men and without fear. For years I dreamed that one day it would be me who would be embraced as Péralte had been, that it would be my body which would receive the sacred ointments, the juices of the *korosôl* we are given to drink as soon as we can hold a glass in our tiny hands. I wanted my soul to be given a proper burial, to be shown the way to *Ginen* so that I could always find my way back, speak to my brothers and sisters at all times.

I am a quiet rebel. I am a teacher. I teach the children left out on the streets to write *créole,* to value themselves, to speak their minds. But still I had hoped that the day my body expired I would be made to live again. But there will be nothing. Not even my mother with her *mambo* hands can bring me back to life. I am her son and it is not natural for a son to lead his mother into the grave.

It was my mother who taught me all the sacred ways, my mother, so soft a heart, so generous a soul. I used to watch her in her garden tilling the soil beneath her rose bushes, oblivious to the world, singing old folk songs quietly to herself. I used to watch how she would plunge her bare hands into the bushes, cutting this branch or that one, shaping it into *obéissance* to have the new buds reveal themselves. The next day, the flowers would open and it would be like staring into the face of Legba's *kataroulo*: the roses a brilliant gold churning like the spokes of a wheel against the green leaves. My mother's hands would glow too, as if they had been touched by a divine presence. It is this I remember most: her hands, smooth like a baby's, brown like honey.

I was young when I left her. Barely eighteen. I wanted to see the world and Papa Léo found a way to get me into the American army. It took me long years of going to sea in metal ships to discover that the army was going to kill me, the same way they had killed the *cacos,* Péralte, even little girls playing in the streets. One day they would be asking me to step onto Haitian shores and kill my own brothers and sisters. I was raising the blue, red, white flag one day and I saw myself as a traitor. *Oui, un traitre.* I was better than that. Yes, better. I left them and came back to my mother. She was still bending over her flowers, tending the soil, gathering grass in bunches to weave small baskets for her seeds. She took me into her arms and said: *Je savais que tu allais revenir.* She took me into the house and showed me a table full of things to eat: *Tu vois, je t'attendais.* It was 1976 and I had been away for about four years. In that time, very little seemed to have changed. I was taken off to jail for questioning as soon as I set foot in Haiti and every few months thereafter. My mother worried to see me gone so often and her mind began to lose its coherent hold on daily life.

I worked for Pot Parol Kreyol and taught whoever wanted to learn. In return, my students taught me to look up from the pages of books and see their faces. They had beautiful eyes, my students. They were full of pain and full of hope and I saw myself in them. My students brought me into the underground and I worked with them to plan the *libération.* My life had purpose. I saw more of Haiti in those three years than I had seen in all of my life before. I was finally home.

By the end of that third year, I found myself utterly lost to my mother, to my students. They could not find me. I had been taken in the middle of the night to a prison where all I heard in the dark around me were moans of pain and screams of anger. I did not know what I was doing there. I had never been in such a place before. I was a patriot, wasn't I? I loved Haiti. I loved the people. I loved myself. I had proven it more than once, every time they had detained me.

They took me to a small room where the floors were sticky with some substance I could not see and they tied me to a chair. At first they asked me questions about my students, our organization, but then they wanted to know about my mother.

She's a mambo, isn't she? they asked. *What are you?*
I am a teacher. That is all.

They kept on and on and all I could think about was my mother's flowers and her hands and how nice it would be to sit in the grass by the side of the house and watch her.

When they took me back to the *cachot* I fell hard against my pallet and the others came to speak to me. I don't know what they said. All I could feel was the pain as they peeled away the shreds of clothing sticking in the cuts on my body, the sting when they poured water over my skin.

That night in the cell I dreamed that my mother was looking for me but I could not speak to her. That was when I knew that I would soon die and my spirit would have no place to rest.

When I am running away from my mother's house to find Alphonse, my younger brother so full of spite but so pure too, I realize that all I have done on this soil is futile. I want him to understand me and I want him to protect me. The Macoutes, yes, they are after me. I hear them coming with bullets in their mouths that they hope will be the ones to rip into my flesh and tear my spirit to shreds. I know they will succeed but still I run. Still I seek out Alphonse. I want to believe he will not forsake me. I want to believe that there is love tying us together, brother to brother. But somewhere within me there is always this feeling of true, true dread. I am searching for the church of my spirit. I fear them, yes, the Macoutes. Yes. Yes. I, Delphi, dangerous one, am afraid. I am running and they are picking up my scent, following the foot-prints I leave behind in the moist earth. I run from my mother's home and down the Port-au-Prince hills and into the main streets of the capital as if I have been set on fire. My brain *is* on fire. I wonder if Péralte felt this way when they came for him with their bullets made to explode the flesh, separate the limbs from the body. My legs are sore from all this running. Was he this way? No, I am not comparing myself to Péralte. It would not be good. It would not be true.

I reach Alphonse's house and I see him through the window, sitting in the kitchen. His back to me. He is so young, so unlike me. Yet, we look a little alike. I saw it earlier today when he came to see mother – in his ears, the shape of his head, the lilt of his smile. The resemblance. Only physical. But somewhere in his heart, he must know me. He must know that we are on the same side, that one day he will be able to love me like I have always loved him. Loved him the day his mother brought him to the house in the country where we used to live – a pink house set away from the road and hidden by *quenêpiers* and coconut trees – for a blessing. I held him for a minute. He was so small but so heavy and I knew he would be able to survive anything. I whispered into his ear: *Jé pa gin bòday.* I was hoping that when he was old enough he could see the world around him clearly.

I watch him from the path leading to the house. It is as if I am dead already. I listen to the wind in the palm trees. A storm is coming. The sound is like the waves of the sea crashing on the shore as the tide rises.

Crashing in my head. Panic.

They are coming after

me

me

me

I run towards the house. My clothes are wet with sweat. I smell like the sea, never-ending salt. My life is knocking on the door. My heart is leaping into my mouth and I am screaming at my brother:

OUVRE POT LA!

OUVRE POT LA!

Trying to reason with him. *I only want a word with you.*

I run round the house. The door is open. When I reach the opening to the inner rooms I am stopped by the screen door. I push against it. It is locked. My heart sinks into the soles of my feet. My feet. Blocks of ice. They are after me. Alphonse will not open the door. But he must. He must. I held him in my arms. Did I not hold him in my arms?

I hear him breathing. I hear him praying. Why is he praying? I am not the devil. The devils are running after me.

His voice talking to me. Finally. I am so very tired. Please. *Why. Open. Don't. The. You. Door. Run.* He says, *Run, why don't you.* I say, *Please, I am so very tired.*

79

The chill. The quiet. The shadow of his body against the wall opposite the door – strange shape, looming.

Yes, they are after me. Alphonse is not my brother.

Blood pumping in my ears, I step away from the house and fall back into the darkness. I must keep a level head. I must not die. I must run very far.

The dawn is breaking by the time I reach *Grande-Saline*. The sky is greyish blue and streaked with long clouds the shape of machetes. The moon hovers above, waiting for the hour of its disappearance. I stand on the beach and listen to the churning of the sea water a few feet in front of me in the dark. I can see only the foam, white froth appearing like magic to soothe my tired eyes. There is hope here, in the water that has taken in its womb the blood of the fallen, swept away the bloated corpses of the vanquished. Yes, hope. The water, clear as a new day, full of promises, waits for us, standing dumb on the shores, to come to terms with all its whisperings.

Behind me I hear the tires of the truck which brought me here spinning against the sand. The motor screeches, splutters and then hums noisily as the driver heads into the city. It was luck that sent the truck my way, pure luck. I do not think that the devils have been able to follow me this far.

The sand is cool beneath my feet, calming. I did not want to be taken all the way to the main street at this hour of the morning. I want peace, a quiet moment. My heart is no longer beating against my rib cage, but my head hurts. So much hurt filling my brain, my ears buzzing.

I call out my mother's name over the sea. It comes back to me in an echo. I know she is somewhere ahead of me, preparing the children for the demonstration they want to hold in St. Raphael, to show that they have a voice too, that they have needs. My *mambo* mother is somewhere out there, painting placards, braiding hair, sewing buttons on scraggly shirts. My *mambo* mother, whom so many despised, accused of ill-doing, was, in truth, working quietly to make life better for others.

Why such fear and hatred of my mother who would never hurt a fly, whose hands were healing tools? I cradle my head in my

80

hands, pressing against the pain, wishing that she were here to soothe it away. Mami Céleste, I say. Mami Céleste. Her voice comes back to me, softly, as when, bent over her flowers, her face away from me, she would say: *Ou sé papiyon, moin sé lanp.* And I know I will find her before there are no suns left for me to see.

The children are assembled in a wild clump of colours, their skins a rainbow of browns shining under the sun. They look up at me with wild anticipation. They are so fearless, so innocent, so beyond my running into the night like a wild person. I look down into their faces and am ashamed of the road it took to bring me here. I am ashamed to look at my mother who is standing far, far from the crowd, as if she is not of it but only an onlooker. The children have brought their brothers and sisters, their parents, the odd grandparent. They hoist placards high above their heads. They chant: *Libèté. Libèté.* They are so proud. They look at me with such pride. I mouth their words, take up the placard they have made for me. It reads: *Ayiti sé tè tout moun.*

We are fearless. We are innocent. We are happy. So beyond running.

Away.

Away.

I lead them through the streets.

Libèté. Libèté.

Rue Pétion. Chemin Dessalines. Boulevard J.F.K.

We are.

So happy.

The wind brushes through us like fire. The placards flap noisily like birds wanting to fly.

I am.

So beyond.

Sweat drips off our foreheads and onto our arms. Pools of water beneath our armpits spread stains through our clothes.

Running.

We are chanting. Running.

Away. Away. Away.

Libèté. Libèté.

And they come. I knew they would come.

I look for my mother and I do not see her. Though I feel her. Nearby.

They come running towards us as we walk down the streets. They are a deep blue like the sky. Dark like rain clouds. They take out their guns and they shoot right through us. Black leather boots walking on our bodies as if we are sacks of coffee beans. Sacks of *charbon*.

The man in front of me. Smiling at me. I smile back, placard balanced against my shoulder. He is so blue. His eyes are like mirrors. Sound of thunder. No noise. So quiet all around me. No pain in my mind, just in my chest. Everything is numb. Falling on my knees. The man pushing past my fall. Mami Céleste gathering me up like a fallen coconut. Dragging me away. Pieces of gravel digging channels down my legs. Mami Céleste looking into my face. Crying tears into my eyes. Her honey hands fluttering around my ears like butterflies. I try to open my mouth, tell her I have come back to her. NOTHING.

NOTHING. NOT A SOUND.

They will drag her away. Put her in a cell with the others. She will weave secret spells around the children so that their spirits will not die. She will purify the fluids of their bodies so that they will have water to drink. She will make an altar to *Fa* below the light coming through the high, barred window and she will chant:

> *Atibo Legba, ouvré pot la pou moin*
> *Papa Legba, ouvré pot la pou moin*
> *Ouvré pot la pou moin kab entré*
> *Kan map tounain dé Vilokan, map salué loas la*
> *Vodou Legba, ouvré pot pou moin*
> *Pou kan moin tounain, map kab mècié loas*
> > *Ayibobo!!*

And I will travel through the mountains, the valleys, to find her at that window. I will come in the form of a dove with one of her roses in my beak. I will let the flower fall through the bars, and when she bends down to take the yellow flower in her hands she will know that I am not lost, that someday all the doors will open. We will be one people. *Libèré*. No longer knocking at the doors built to keep us silent.

PART TWO

ALPHONSE'S STORY

CHAPTER ONE

America is like a slick picture postcard which tells of endless stretches of unspoiled beauty and quiet, starlit evenings. America lifts you out of a deep slumber with the aroma of a strong cup of morning coffee to launch you into the adventure of a new day, which is the life you wish you had. America is like a beckoning mermaid in the middle of the ocean staring out at you from the pages of glossy magazines with her long fingers and perfect smile. America is a dream.

Alphonse had dreamed of going to America through years of buying *Time Magazine*, and the TV guide in which the listings did not match the Haitian network, but tell of wondrous happenings like the bombing of metro centers and the good fortune of people down on their luck winning brand new cars on the game shows. Alphonse liked to keep in touch with the country which had dominated his own for so long, to know who the big stars were, to know the latest gizmos for opening cans of tuna, and the strength of the U.S. currency against his own *gourdes* – which were fast becoming worthless like the cents one throws in fish ponds at resort hotels. His stack of magazines, as high as his hip, lay under the desk M'sieur Léo had put in his room some years ago when he had announced that Alphonse would go on to high school as his mother had wished. But then came the year of her illness and M'sieur Léo decided to pay her bills with Alphonse as bond– he would have to repay with his life it seemed, in endless servitude.

Alphonse had hated M'sieur Léo ever since he had been brought to live in this house in the hills, surrounded by its high, whitewashed walls and sneering, headless bottles. He had wanted to stay in the countryside where everything seemed better – the air, the water, even the small schoolhouse that the wealthy side of the village had threatened to tear down, saying it was an eyesore and a disgrace. Hated M'sieur Léo even more when, on the night he cried, huddled against his mother, begging her to take him home, she had whispered quietly into his hair: "*M'sieur Léo sé pè ou. Li pra rend vi ou plu facil.*" How could his father force him to be a servant in his own home? It made a bitter taste in his mouth, like tasting spoiled meat by mistake. He had cried; he had wanted to say that he would take his old life back with pleasure. That day, he decided he would never cry again if he could help it. He was seven that year, and like the French boy characters of long ago he had read about in stories for school, he had become a man. He had left his mother, worked for his keep, and wore long pants in defiance of the summer heat.

Alphonse watched the other children who came to the house with mixed feelings of interest and resentment. One, Josèphe, he knew, was his cousin, the other, Désirée, might as well have been for all the time she spent there when her parents were away. He thought it strange that he did not have brothers and sisters in the house, but M'sieur Léo's wife said she wanted her freedom, and children would only keep her entrapped in a marriage that, also strangely he thought, she did not seem to want to be freed from. Sometimes she would call him up to her room and talk to him about how her life had been before the elaborate wedding in Port-au-Prince to Léo. Her speech would be a garble of slurred words. When Alphonse got older and was made to dust parts of the house like the cleaning women, he realized that she was always drinking. He swept away empty bottles of Rum Barbancourt into paper sacks and set them against the curb outside the high walls. When the other children came Madam would often hide in her room with the door locked, as if she was afraid of catching an incurable disease. On those days, the children could do what they liked, and Alphonse would wander away from the house without having to worry too much about his chores. The older women, especially the cook Bella, would pick up the slack for him.

Josèphe was younger than he was, but he got along with her all right. Age didn't matter much when there was little choice. Désirée, being closer in age, was a co-conspirator; Jo was like their baby sister, a pest at times, a marvellous toy at others, on whom they could play tricks or force to be braver than she was at so young an age. Alphonse did not know how to relate to the little girl who resembled him in the lost look of her eyes and the outward curve of her thumbs. She always seemed afraid of something, and he thought of her as someone who, having led a sheltered and pain-free life, was afraid of any change in the pattern. Josèphe came to the island on summer vacations and he had seen her growing taller and thinner, into the woman she would become in that far away place he resented her most for: America. Always America. It stood between them, who were of the same blood, as an invisible wall that had to do with money and a name. Her name could unlock doors, his would keep him imprisoned in the crevices below the house, scuttling like an ugly cockroach trying to escape sunlight, trying to survive the crunch of a boot upon his back.

America. The word bound in his mind like a wistful promise. A-me-ri-ca. Alphonse sat on the thin mattress, which had been his bed for these many years, and thumbed through the latest sports magazine Cousin Eric, who worked for the President's secret police, had given him. Maybe, once he got to America, he could become one of these celebrated men. He did not consider that, at twenty-six, he was already too old to achieve some of the dreams he'd clung to since childhood.

There came a knock at the door. Alphonse closed the magazine slowly, taking a last look at the pictures, windows to his every hope, and went to open the door, which was barely a door, just a few pieces of varnished plywood hammered together and suspended on hinges. The lock was a hook which could easily be broken, so he always left it unhinged as if to tempt fate to do more harm to him than it had already done.

M'sieur Léo stood on the other side of the door, rubbing pudgy hands together in agitation. His heavy frame took up the whole of the door space. Beads of perspiration glistened in his beard and his eyes had the glassy look of a man who had been up for days or drinking heavily. "I have bad news I must tell you," he said.

86

Alphonse gripped the door tightly and braced himself, as he had done five years earlier when M'sieur Léo had appeared unflustered at the door, uttered those same words, and handed him an envelope stuffed with a little money from his mother. Then, M'sieur had come to tell him that his mother was dead – as casually as if a cow had died or a goat been slaughtered for the evening meal!

"My mother has died," M'sieur said. He rubbed his now balding head and brought his hands to rest against the door frame, as if a huge weight was threatening to press him into the ground. "I know you were close to her, so I thought you should know." His voice faltered and he began to cry. He reached for Alphonse and embraced him as he had never done in all the years Alphonse had been a child in need of physical contact with his father, in need of any contact really that would make him feel alive and a part of the human race.

Alphonse's body shook in the strong arms that held him close against his will. He felt angry and vulnerable all at once. He wanted to cry for his grandmother with her son, but he also felt like pummelling his father's back with hard blows. He wished that M'sieur Léo had died instead. Léo mistook the movement for grief and held onto his son more tightly, as if this one, brief connection could wipe out the past.

"There will be things to do," Alphonse said into M'sieur Léo's shoulder. He tried to pull away. "We must attend to things."

"Of course," M'sieur let him go. "Of course you are right."

In a moment it seemed that M'sieur had forgotten his agitation and spilling of tears. He stood straight in the doorway and listed all the things that Alphonse would have to get ready. He made Alphonse repeat everything he said, as if he was a small child who would easily forget instructions. And then he walked up the stairs and into the house, leaving his son behind, as if Alphonse himself could never ascend those stairs and take his rightful place beside his father at the dining room table.

His grandmother's passing was the closing of a chapter for Alphonse. There did not seem to be a reason for crying or despairing or even trying to make sense of the loss. It seemed that the loss had happened long ago, before he was even born, on the night his mother and father had conceived him, but neglected to think ahead. He was not sorry that he'd been born, only sorry that he'd had to live hidden away from his mother's shame, in his father's loathing.

At the beginning, the days he spent in his mother's house were times of relief. He would come home at the end of the week and his mother would take him in her arms and squeeze him tight and ask: "How is my lettuce head, my little avocado heart?" She would stop him from answering. "I'm so fine, Mami," she would say in a high-pitched, sing-song voice. "What do you have good for me to eat?"

He would play along, trying to forget how tired he was from a day of peeling potatoes in a bucket between his knees, or cutting and cleaning okra for a stew, and repeat her question: "Mami, what do you have for me?"

Delighted, Mami would hurry him into the kitchen and seat him down as if he was king of the castle. "You are going to be happy with your Mami," she would call back to him as she opened the door of the modern gas range M'sieur Léo had given her, as if the luxury of the cooking appliance would compensate for the absence of her son. She might bring back a thin, flat cake of *pâté* and he would tear greedily into the flaky, honeyed crust to reach the finely milled meats inside. Their scent filled his nostrils and mouth with the most fragrant spices, transporting him back to times when he worried about nothing but what might be the next delicious meal.

But after some time, as his shirts seemed to shrink about his waist and the collars gripped the thickening muscles of his neck, Alphonse noticed that he had started to walk more slowly down the hill away from the big houses to the simple house on the outskirts of town where his mother lived. Alphonse grew tall and strong; his face lost its roundness, turning into the shape of a banana leaf – with sharply rising cheekbones – and he took to sporting a thin line of hair on his upper lip – like his father. Only his ears still protruded as they had done when he was a small boy and his mother would rub them as he ate, as if a genie was hidden there who would give her back her little son. Alphonse began to resent her as he felt the self he actually was becoming more and more invisible to her. Now the food she placed before him seemed tasteless; the bright colours of the pastries and fruits were like the beautiful panels of paintings he had seen hanging in M'sieur Léo's house, not for touching, beautiful but unreal. And while he was no longer prepared to play along with her game, he thought that his mother still talked to him and to herself as if all their conversations had taken place already in her mind and she was only reliving them when he came home.

One weekend when he came home he had to walk through the house to find her. The kitchen was full of dirty dishes and black ants the size of penny candy were crawling through the wreckage. The sheets on her bed were twisted together in a long and dingy white cord and the house was stuffy. The window shades, which she usually left wide open, even in the middle of the night when burglars were apt to come by, were tightly shut. He found her sitting in the back yard on an old chair surrounded by foot-high grass. She was in the same pale pink nightdress she had been wearing at the beginning of the week when she'd waved goodbye to him from the front stoop, rocking back and forth in her red and black leather slippers as if to soothe the dull ache of seeing him go once again.

"Is that you, *cher?*" Her voice crooned to him like a distant bird's. Alphonse, recalling the drunk woman he had just left in his father's house, feared the worst.

"Is that you, Léo?"

The sound of his father's name fell like a sharp blow in his chest. Alphonse stopped walking, suspended breathing. The cocoa, orange and papaya smells of the back yard rushed into his head like a possessing spirit, torturing him with a familiarity he did not want associated with *that* man. His hands, long like his grandmother's, made for shaping wood into serviceable pieces of furniture, balled themselves into fists. "*Mami? Ou pren rêvé?*"

"*Ein? Vin ici, Léo, pou ma kab tandé parol dous ou.*"

"Ma-mi," Alphonse's voice broke with pain, "*sé Alphi ki la, oui.*" He walked towards his mother, fearing who she would see when he came closer. He put both his hands on her shoulders and felt her muscles jump as she reached to cover them with her own. He was surprised at how thin they were, how fragile. These were hands which had carried him into the city when she had gone to sell her goods at market, hands which had milled wheat into flour to make bread, which had held the heavy loads she balanced on the jutting sharpness of her hip on the days she worked for herself, taking care of the laundry and cooking.

"*Moin conten ou la,*" his mother said quietly.

He smiled, the fear beginning to lift from his shoulders like the remnants of a bad dream after waking.

"Léo," she said, "*Sé ou coeu' coeu' moin.*"

Alphonse stood behind his mother, not wanting to do anything which would startle or upset her. Slowly he removed his hands from beneath hers and came to crouch in front of the chair, steadying himself between her legs as he had done when he was a child and she smoothed oil into his scalp to make it shine. He took her hands which had fallen back into her lap and held them against his face. "*Gadé'm, Mami,*" he said. "It's me. It's Alphi. *Bébé ou.*"

He looked into her eyes and what he saw staring back scared him. They were dry and lifeless, like an empty coconut husk. If they held memories of his childhood days, they lurked in some shadowy corner. He could see no reflection of himself. Then, as a soft wind alighted upon them both, her vision cleared. "Ah, *oui,*" she said and smiled weakly, "it is you, Alphi. You have come back already? How is everything with you?"

Alphonse could not respond. Tears threatened to spill from his eyes but he fought them back. "Mami," he whispered, "Mami." His mother only smiled, with her head perched to the side like a curious bird, and she stroked his head as if he were still small and needed comforting.

They sat in the dark through the night, Alphonse not daring to move, his mother lost in her faraway thoughts. It was morning when Alphonse noticed that there was a picture in his mother's lap, overturned to reveal a shaky handwriting on the back. It read: "*A Léo, avec tout mon amour, Céleste.*"

Alphonse looked up from the words on the photograph to his mother, whose eyes had closed, giving in to a deep slumber. He took the photograph from her lap and turned it over. A man who resembled him looked out of the photograph with a closed face and veiled eyes. He wore a light cotton suit and a shirt tied tightly at the base of his neck with a long, thin necktie. The cuffs of the shirt protruded from the arms of the jacket to reveal gold cufflinks in the shape of military stars that he knew all too well. He could hardly believe how young the man looked, how much like himself, without the protruding stomach his father now had, and with a full head of hair. A small woman was seated next to the man, much as his mother now sat before him, hands locked together in her lap, legs crossed and hidden beneath the fabric of a long skirt. But it was not his mother. The woman's face was rounder. Her head seemed small above the wideness of a full chest. Her eyes were round like grapes. She, too, was not smiling. It looked like the picture of a married couple.

How could this be? His father and yet another woman in such an apparently permanent arrangement. Though they seemed stiff and lifeless before the camera's eye, the figures looked at ease together, with the look of two people who had known each other perhaps too long, too well. But if the mysteries of their hearts' breathless, tentative early years had been discarded, they had left behind a bond, hollow but strong, that neither could deny. The picture had been taken in a studio: the background was nondescript, a washed-out grey that could have been a wall or a hanging sheet.

He was still trying to make sense of the picture when his mother awoke. She saw the photograph in his hand, snatched it from him and slid it into the pocket of her night dress. She closed her eyes and ignored him until she could hear his feet pressing down the tall grass as he walked away.

Alphonse spent most of the morning tidying the house: cleaning the dishes, making the beds, sweeping the floors. He made bowls of hot *acassan* for their lunch with fresh sliced bananas spread on top, mixing in sweetness with salt to soothe the sting of the long night's vigil. He thought that it would be an easy meal for his mother to eat.

For a moment Alphonse sat alone at the table before calling Mami. He placed his hands on its rough wood surface, marked with water stains and knife nicks, the table to which he had been led so lovingly after long tiring weeks, when the days were just a jumble of hours of light followed by hours of darkness. His body now felt the same pull of exhaustion, the muscles like cords that had been stretched too far and placed back beneath a skin that no longer had room for them. There was a pain in his head he could not quite locate: it moved like a slow worm tunnelling from behind his forehead, along the sides of his head above his ears. Alphonse closed his eyes against the pain, but it only brought him closer to the pain rather than away from it. He opened his eyes and looked out of the back door to his mother who still had not moved from her chair. He wondered how it must feel to live in her body, all the woman-things that went on that he would never know. "Mami?" he called out to her, his voice flat but soft with love for this woman who had tried to make his life more bearable. "*Mami. Vin ici. Tan pou mangé, oui.*"

"*Map vini.*" Her voice fluttered into the house on a warm breeze, but she did not appear to have moved. Her head was turned away from the house, looking far out into the pale sky. A chill shook Alphonse as he watched his mother finally rise from the chair to make her way to the house.

As she walked into the kitchen, leather slippers slapping against the linoleum tiles, her whole body seemed to be dragging itself from one step to the next. Alphonse had not noticed before how much his mother had aged. She was no longer the woman he had fallen in love with when he was six years old and childishly vowed to marry. In his sight, she had walked on air and he saw how all the men would practically bend in two to make her compliments and help her with her loads. She, though, would refuse or ignore them, depending on her mood, walking on as if no load could be too much for her. There had always been a mischievous smile waiting at the corners of her mouth. Now there was nothing. Alphonse could barely make out the outline of her lips which seemed to have melted into the leathery brown of her skin. There were deep, dark crescents beneath her eyes the colour of coffee grounds that no amount of sleep could take away. Her once lithe figure had become thick and lumpy with knots that jutted through her clothing. Her skin was ashen, no longer luminous with the mysterious glow that came from beneath the surface .

She stood at the side of the table and stared at her son with a fire in her eyes he had seldom seen.

"What is it?" he asked, "I made us something to eat. Something to make you feel better. Don't you think that. . ."

"Here," she interrupted him abruptly, "you wanted to see it. Here it is." She took the picture from her pocket and flung it face up on the table.

"Mami, I don't want to see it. I've seen it."

"*Oui. Oui.* You want to see it. You shall see it."

"But Mami." Alphonse just wanted all this to be over. He wanted her to eat and get back the strength he knew her for. "Come and sit. Eat."

"No." She took the picture from the table and held it up to him. "You see this woman? Look at her carefully." Alphonse looked away. "She could be the woman you look after in M'sieur Léo's house today. An-han. Yes, you look at her. You don't recognize the face?" Alphonse looked back at the woman in the photograph and tried to guess.

"I don't know, Mami. That picture is so old. What does it matter now?"

A long laugh came from his mother's throat which made his skin crawl. It was the laugh of a woman who was filled with poison. It bruised his ears with its bilious sound. "Mami," he said, "Mami. Please. Let go of it."

As if he referred to the photograph, his mother's hand closed tightly around it, crumpling it within her fist. "No," she said. "I will tell you. You see me now as I am, *einh* ? An old, old woman. I was not always this way. Your father, he loved me. He loved *me*. We had you and everything would have been all right even though he was married. But then, there was *her*. Céleste with all her *mambo* jambo." She cackled. "Yes, it's true. She is a *mambo*. They say she deals with the good spirits, but she brought me only pain and hardship. You see me, Alphi? She has put a curse on me. A curse!"

"What do you mean, Mami? Come now. It's all in the past." Alphonse waved his hands around his mother, as if shooing away bad spirits instead of flies. He wanted her to forget about this, but the name Céleste had jarred him to remember the woman everyone called Mademoiselle Dominique. She had lived near his grandmother's house until M'sieur Léo had moved her further away after all her children were grown. Then she had lived in the hills and gained a reputation as a magic-worker ever since she had emerged unscathed from a fire lit in her house by another jealous *métres* of Tonton Léo's, particularly when the other woman had died of a painful smallpox . So the rumours were true.

He watched his mother clutch at her arms as if small ticks were biting her flesh and felt the stirrings of a revulsion he had never felt towards her before.

"Ah, Alphi. You don't know. You don't know." She sat down at the table, hugging herself, her eyes cloudy with tears.

"Mami." Alphonse pushed the bowl of *acassan* he had made for her across the table and poured a little lake of milk in the centre. "Come. It's time to eat."

His mother laughed at the bowl. "I don't know what you put in there." She squinted at him and dropped her voice to a whisper. "She has been here, you know. You shouldn't make food here. It could be poisoned. Look." She took out a jumble of string and hair from her pocket. The lump had the pungent smell of manure.

Alphonse grimaced. "Throw it out."

"Ah-ah! How can you say that?" She shook it above the table and clumps of dirt fell into her bowl of *acassan*. "It is proof is it not? She pulled at the hairs surrounding the dirt. "This is *my* hair. Mine. What is it doing in this? It's a curse I tell you."

"Where did you find it?" Alphonse doubted his mother's words. That lump could be anything, from anywhere.

"It was back there, in the yard. I found it when I was walking through the grass. She didn't even bother to hide it."

Alphonse began to recall how he, Josèphe, and Désirée had spent afternoons making up games to bother Mlle. Dominique. He remembered the day they sent Jo after one of her roses and Mlle. Dominique had not seemed herself but more like a crazy woman. Alphonse looked at his mother again. In truth, the two women were much the same, loving the same loathsome man, letting him use them up then throw them aside when he found someone new, and living for their children only when it was too late and both their children had left them behind to pursue dreams that seemed sweeter and more promising than looking after their aging mothers. "Mami," he said, "Mlle. Dominique is old like you. She doesn't need to do this. M'sieur Léo doesn't pay her any more attention than he does to..." he stopped himself, not wanting to utter the obvious. "She hasn't been right in the head for years. *De toute façon*, she isn't well enough or strong enough to come all the way here."

"Ay! Alphi!" His mother shook her head in disbelief. "Don't you know spirits have wings, the good and the bad?" With that she slipped the crumbling lump of hair, soil and manure back into her pocket. Alphonse made a mental note to look for it later and throw it out. Then he cleared the table, taking the bowls of porridge out to the pigs his mother kept in a pen in a far corner of the yard. He was sixteen and there was nothing else he knew to do.

After that morning, Alphonse spent many long days going back and forth between the city house and his mother's country home where she lay sick and dying. His father, by contrast, except for his loss of hair, seemed to be growing both larger around his middle and in wealth. The muscles of her arms had become cords of flabby flesh like worn elastic. A virus was eating away at her from the inside, but she persisted in believing that she'd had a curse put on her by Mademoiselle Dominique. She lay wasting away on her bed and refused to move, even when the doctors told her it might be her only hope. Every time Alphonse passed through the doorway of the house, she would begin to speak to the Lord and ask forgiveness: "*Si ou vlé moin, Bondye, m'ap vini. Sé pou ou ke m'ap vi. Sé pou ou seul.*"

Every time Alphonse heard those words he would curse her in his heart, wondering why his name was never on her lips, why she did not want to live for him.

The day he walked in the door and her familiar words did not greet him, Alphonse knew that she was gone. And for a long time, he asked himself how the photograph of Mlle. Dominique and M'sieur Léo had found its way into his mother's hands. It had broken her spirit and, with it, all his surviving hopes.

CHAPTER TWO

After his mother's death, Alphonse thought constantly about Mlle. Dominique. His mother's obsession with the quiet woman who lived down the street from his father's place in a small but colourful house – the outer walls painted rust red and ochre blue – became his own. He carried the picture his mother had flung on the kitchen table the day she had mistaken him for his father in his trouser pocket. He tried to make sense of his mother's accusation that Mlle. Dominique had put her under a spell. Mlle. Dominique looked so delicate in the picture it was impossible to imagine that she was the *mambo* she had been rumoured to be for so many years – able to make grown men cry and even the *madanm-saras* fear.

Every day, after taking care of peeling and cutting the vegetables and fruits for Bella to prepare for supper, he would find a quiet corner to sit and contemplate the picture of Mlle. Dominique and his father. He thought that sooner or later it would reveal some sign of what he should do. He did not know if he should avenge his mother's death, or if her passing was itself a sign that he needed to do something with his life and that this would put things right again.

"What do you have there?" Bella asked him one day as she came down the stairs to join him on the wooden bench in front of their sleeping quarters.

Alphonse looked at Bella and wondered what she would think of his mother if he showed her the photograph. He knew it would fuel her hatred of M'sieur Léo so he handed it to her. "*'Tention,*" he said, "*M'pa gin lôt.*"

"*Bon, Bon.*" Bella took the picture in her large hands and held it in front of her as if it was a strange object she had just unearthed from an archaeological dig. She peered at the figures in the photograph, suddenly pulled her head back and let out a loud guffaw. "*Ay. Ay,*" she said. "He has no shame that one."

Alphonse knew she spoke of M'sieur Léo and his chest tightened with an inexplicable feeling of shame. The picture made real what everyone knew about his father, that he was a crude man with pretentious social aspirations, that he would hurt anyone without a second thought if it was to his advantage. Alphonse was thinking of his mother's constant sorrow, but it occurred to him that M'sieur Léo's wife must have lived with this shame all through their marriage. For once he felt a pang of compassion for her, thinking how broken a spirit she seemed when she drowned herself in drink.

"Give it back to me."

"No. No. Don't be so sensitive. Let me appreciate the beauty. This is a treasure." Bella started to laugh again, the kind of laugh he heard coming out of bars late at night in the capital when he walked home, always tempted with the prospect of sitting in one of them with people who had come from the continent to stare at him and tell him how beautiful he was. He wanted to know what it was like to be one of those men who could pull out wads of greenbacks, slap them down on the bamboo counter and yell in bad French with a thick American accent: "*Une tour pour toute le monde!*" The people crowded in the hot and smoky room would forget that he was just a poor boy from the country as he drew in the men with the pale skins to drink alongside men with the sun warmed into theirs. He would hear the cheer go up around him: "*Hop-la!*" But his feet kept moving swiftly along the road. Was it because he wasn't yet really a man and because fear gripped him at the thought of the women in the bars looking at him with moist and milky eyes, licking their rouged lips as if they were a sticky sweet worth his effort to taste?

Alphonse snatched the picture from Bella's hands. "You can have some respect for the dead. You are laughing in my mother's ears. I swear she'll hear you. *Bondye* help you if she does."

Bella covered her mouth with her hands, one on top of the other. Her eyes were half-closed with merriment, wrinkles flowing from them towards the base of her hairline. A lock of hair fell loose from the bun she wore on the top of her head; it bobbed up and down in front of her nose and tickled her. She began to hiccup loudly, her plump body shaking all over like a jelly refusing to set on a hot day.

Alphonse could only feel disgust. "This is not for your amusement."

"But it is." Bella tried to suppress a hiccup and it sounded like a frog croaking in her throat. "It is. Your father is a joke."

"An-han," Alphonse sneered. "And you are laughing at Mlle. Dominique too. You know what they say about her."

Bella quickly sobered at this thought. Many years ago, Mlle. Dominique had almost become the mistress of the house. Bella had never liked the quiet woman who cultivated roses and hibiscus along the sides of her house as if she was trying to build a shield of colour and fragrance, as if she was someone special. "Yes, I know what they say about her and it's true. I have a cousin from l'Artibonite who used to come to see me when I first started here. She was very young." Bella paused, her honey coloured skin becoming pale. Her voice broke in odd places as she spoke: "It. Yes. It was. Long ago. I remember all so well how. My cousin Ma. Her name was. Mathilde. Yes that is. What it was. So we called her Ma. For short. The story is like this, like this. She would come to see me when she did not. Have to go to school. Yes. That was why. To help me. Her mother sent her to. Help. Yes. And M'sieur took a liking to. Her. Wanted her. You could see it in his eyes the way. He took her in. Like a demon he was. All that time. She never said anything to me. Until. Until it was too late and she was. With child. Mlle. Dominique was called. She was very angry. Yes. Angry is what I would say. They yelled at each other for a long time. Madame was away in Kenscoff that weekend. And when Madame came back, Ma was no longer with child. Mlle. Dominique had given her something. From a jar. It smelled. Ma's skin had the smell of spoiled meat to it for months after. And he never touched her after that. Mlle. Dominique said she would kill him if he did. The picture explains everything. Every. Thing. If only. Ma. If only. She had told me. I could have. I could…" Bella's voice gave out, as if she had been holding back this story for far too long.

"When did this happen?" Alphonse felt a sudden pressing need to find out everything to be learned about his father.

Bella's eyes were closed and she was humming to herself. "It was long ago. But not so very long." Her voice seemed disembodied, her lips barely moved. She rocked back and forth on the bench.

"How long, Bella?" Alphonse softened his voice. "Tell me how long."

"Ten years. Around the time M'sieur had Mlle. Dominique brought here from the country when her son Delphi joined the Marines."

Alphonse counted back. It would have been around 1972 and he would have been six, still living in the country with Mami. He could not remember anything happening out of the ordinary. He slipped the picture back into his pocket and decided that after his afternoon chores were done he would pay a visit to Mlle. Dominique. He was not afraid. He would confront her whether she was good or evil. If she had put a curse on his mother he needed to know. He left his hand wrapped around the picture in his pocket for a while; he did not want Bella to see his hand shaking in anger as she would if he removed it. "Don't you have to get back to work?" he asked, trying to move her away from him. "They'll wonder where you've gone."

Bella pulled back her shoulders and sat up straight. She enjoyed sitting here with Alphonse. He was a quiet boy and she liked him. Even though their quarters were small and cramped, they were cooler than the rest of the house. She liked to sit in the shade and feel the damp coolness of the earthen floor. It made her feel peaceful to be away from the oven heat and the demands of M'sieur Léo and his wife. "No," Bella sighed, "they would have screamed for me by now. But yes, I should go. The sooner I go, the sooner I can come back."

Alphonse spent the afternoon thinking about how he would approach Mlle. Dominique. He did not know what it would feel like to stare into the face creviced with age and see there the young woman who had sat, so docile, by his father's side years ago. He did not know what it would be like to stare into that face with the knowledge that the woman who looked so frail was really as strong as a cane stalk, resisting being cut down. He swept the sprawling dining and living rooms, the upstairs bedrooms. He even retraced his steps to the kitchen to sweep up for Bella, to make her load a little lighter. He felt he had made her day harder than it already was, for no real reason. But, he avoided her, not wanting to feel guilt for having made her remember a past it was clear she would sooner forget. He wondered about "Ma" and what had become of her. If she'd had a child, it would have been a half-sister or brother for him. He would have liked a brother.

Finally, it was time for him to gather his things and go home. He hurried out so that no one could detain him to take care of a task that could wait until morning. With his bag flung across his chest he ran from the house yelling: "*A demain!*" He was safely out of sight when he heard Bella calling: "Alphi? Alphi! Where has that boy gone?"

He felt very brave until he reached Mlle. Dominique's gate which had been left open and creaking on its rusty hinges. The once beautiful beds of flowers had been overrun with entangling vines. The grass was tall, burnt to a red-brown in patches. The path leading to the house was hidden from sight, and suddenly Alphonse felt that it would be a frightful journey to get from the street to the rickety porch. He could not tell if Mlle. Dominique was home. He began to whistle nervously.

He took a deep breath and pushed the swinging gate out of his way. He looked with concern as his legs disappeared from view in the long grass that crowded in on him from all sides. He sensed spirits hiding among the overgrown bushes and trees laden with overripe fruits, some of which had fallen rotting in the grass.

When he reached the porch, he took a deep breath and smiled to himself. He ran his hands down his legs and slapped them both. He was all there. All there. He let out a self-conscious laugh. Now he had to see who was home. He knocked on the front door and waited. There was no answer. Boldly, he tried the handle of the door, turned it and found it was unlocked. A *mambo,* of course, has nothing to fear, not even robbers.

He stepped into the house. He had never been inside, not even when he had come with Josèphe and Désirée to play tricks on the old woman.

The house was cluttered, but ordinary, clean, not unlike his grandmother's house.

"What are you doing here?" The voice was low, calm. A man's voice. *"Tandé'm* ? What do you want?"

Alphonse turned around. A man was sitting on the edge of a bed in a room to the right of the main door. Alphonse could only make out the stripes of his shirt, which looked to be green or yellow and shimmered in the dark. The man rose from the bed and walked towards him. He was wearing belted khaki shorts and leather sandals with braided clasps. "I say: what do you *want*?" There was an edge to the voice, as if he had been sleeping and been startled.

Alphonse did not think of himself as an intruder. Rather, he wanted to know who this man was who had the same eyes as he had, the same protruding ears. The man was much taller, broader in the shoulders, with skin the colour of eggplants. Alphonse wanted to reach out to touch him. He felt so very close to him, but he had lost his sense of timing, his sense of when and how he could touch someone and make a connection. "I. . ." His voice faltered. Why *had* he come? Then he remembered the photograph. He tried to meet the man's height, to look him straight in the eye. "I am looking for Mademoiselle Dominique. Is she here?" Alphonse looked around as if it was perfectly natural to enter a stranger's house uninvited and unannounced.

"Who are you?" the man asked.

"It doesn't matter who I am. I want to see Mademoiselle Dominique."

The man shrugged as if to say that he didn't care who Alphonse was either. "You'll be waiting for a long time. You can write your name on that piece of paper and I'll give it to her." He pointed to a pad of paper left on the kitchen counter with a stubby pencil next to the phone.

Alphonse stared at the phone. It hadn't occurred to him that a *mambo* would need a phone.

The man followed his gaze. "You can write, can't you?"

"Of course," Alphonse heard himself say, too quickly. He felt defensive and unsure of himself. He decided to ignore the piece of paper to show that he did not need to prove himself. "My name is Alphonse. Alphonse Lamose."

"Lamose? La-mose." The man rolled the name in his mouth as if he was discovering a rare fruit. "Yes. I know who you are."

"That's good," Alphonse replied. "But I don't know who you are."

The man put out his hand. "Delphi. Delphi Dominique. My enemies call me D.D. My mother calls me Delphi. You can do the same."

Alphonse took the man's hand and shook it. The hand was unusually soft but the grip was strong. Alphonse had the feeling that he had met himself, older, in this man who could be none other than his brother. This thought made his head hot and the purpose of his visit evaporated as he felt this man's skin against his own, like a warm glove on a cool night. He smiled at the man.

"Why do you smile? You don't know who I am."

Confused, Alphonse tried to stop smiling but he could not. "You are my brother."

Delphi let his hand fall. "I suppose I am. But that doesn't mean you should trust me."

Alphonse felt his ears grow hot from the feeling of having been cut down to size. He wanted to prove that he was not a child, that he too could be a man with a slow and steady speech, a becoming coolness. He wanted to know what it would be like to be so sure of himself.

"Why do you want to see my mother?" Delphi asked, and turned away to take two glasses and a bottle of rum from the side counter.

The image of his mother lying prone in her bed, calling out for *Bondye,* still clutching the picture of Mlle. Dominique and M'sieur Léo came back to Alphonse. "She has to answer to me for my mother's death." He was surprised that Delphi did not laugh.

Delphi looked at Alphonse with concern in his eyes. "My mother would never hurt a living thing. Not even an ant." He came close to Alphonse and handed him one of the glasses. "Not even you."

They sat in silence for a long time. Alphonse assumed they were waiting for Delphi's mother – for this was how he thought of her now – to come home. He took his time, sipping at the rum in his glass, watching Delphi's Adam's apple bob up and down as he gulped his rum a glass at a time. He looked at the photographs on the tables at each end of the couch. Mlle. Dominique looked so ordinary with six children crowded around her. He felt there was nothing to fear.

As his gaze strayed about the room, Alphonse's eyes fell on a photograph in a carved, silver frame. It was the same as the one still brushing against his leg in his pocket. He was brought back to the purpose of his visit. He rose from his seat and handed Delphi his glass. "I cannot wait any longer."

"You've just gotten here."

Alphonse felt a pang of guilt. He was surprised by the pleading look in Delphi's eyes. Why did he feel such responsibility for a man he had only just met, knew only through the stories told about his faraway trips? He had expected a man who needed nothing.

Delphi walked back into the room where Alphonse had first found him. "Let me show you something."

Alphonse followed his half-brother into the room and was surprised to find it neatly organized, but overflowing with papers with squiggly lines in blue and black ink. He could not tell what they were. They did not seem to be maps but there were dots marked on each, with the names of cities and villages he knew lay to the north of the capital.

Delphi pulled out a chair from behind a large desk and motioned Alphonse to sit. Then he put one of the sheets of paper in front of Alphonse and smoothed it flat with his hands. The paper was thin like rice paper and the blue lines drawn on it were like veins finding their way across the white surface. "These are maps for the *libération*," Delphi said. He pointed to a dot in the far left corner marked Grande-Saline. "Here, we have been keeping provisions. If anything goes wrong, we can flee towards the continent from here." He pointed to another dot, a little higher and to the right, marked St. Raphael. "Near here, we will be demonstrating."

"What for?" Alphonse interrupted, feeling for the first time more afraid of Delphi than he had been of Mlle. Dominique. It was one thing to be practising magic, quite another to be a subversive. Anything could happen to you. One day you could be walking down the road, whistling to yourself, watching the

103

bananas fall from the trees, and the next day you could find yourself waking to the smell of urine and the noise of men coughing uncontrollably on stained pallets. Then you would begin to make out the bloodstained walls, the dust hanging heavy in the air, and you would know that you had been jailed without trial or reason. Alphonse felt the back of his shirt sticking to the chair. He was sweating even though the room was cool. He wanted to be gone.

"Don't look so fearful, *brother.*" Delphi said the last word with emphasis, to mean that he wanted to believe that Alphonse was part of the cause. "We don't kill. And we don't want to rule. We want to give power back to the people, where it belongs. I know it sounds trite." Delphi lifted the paper carefully from the table and rolled it into a tight, tight stick. "I work with a group from Canada. For literacy. I teach young people like you how to read and write and look ahead."

"I know how to read and how to write. In Créole and in French."

Delphi nodded. "I know. Didn't I say that I know who you are? But do you know how to look ahead?"

Alphonse rose from the chair. "*Gadé.* I didn't come here for you. I came here for your mother."

"You have to let all of that go. It means nothing."

"Your mother killed mine."

"Surely you don't believe such nonsense."

"I believe what I know. My mother died in agony. Your mother is alive and living in this house M'sieur Léo gave to her."

"Who told you that?"

"I just know."

Delphi placed the map in a corner of the room with other tubed papers. He lay down on the bed and ignored Alphonse.

Alphonse stared at Delphi in disbelief. What was he to do now? He walked out of the room feeling discouraged and baffled at this man who seemed to want peace and revolution hand in hand. He was almost out the door when Delphi's voice reached him: "Your mother was a broken woman. She saw what she wanted to see."

Night had enveloped the capital in a quilt of smoke and ashes blowing in the breeze as meagre dinners were cooked over open flames in the *lakou-foumi*. The thatched-roof buildings were so cramped together that sometimes they caught fire when the cook's back was turned. But this was not one of those nights. The smell of roasting pork and boiling rice rose above the roof tops and lingered there. There was a sound like rain mingling with the smells – the sound of people talking to each other, catching up on their days and bringing them to a close in the light of the cooking fires.

Alphonse walked through the crowded roads, muttering what he hoped was the Lord's prayer – *Jésus ayez pitié de moi* – stepping over the flow of dirty water which ran freely in the streets – *Notre Père qui est au cieux* – filled with rotting foods and excrement – *Priez pour nous pauvres pêcheurs*. The stench wormed itself into his nose – *Que ton nom soit sanctifié* – but he ignored it – *Que ton règne vienne*. His mind was in a knot he was desperate to undo – *que ta volonté sois faite*. He wanted to kill both Mlle. Dominique and Delphi. *Priez pour moi, seigneur.* He wanted to be free of them both.

When he reached his mother's house, Alphonse felt relief wash over him like a soft breeze. He was comforted at the sight of the old furniture, the kitchen table with its nicks and water marks, everything in its place, just as he had left it a week ago. He threw open the shutters to let in the night air and breathed deeply. Even though the house was not far from the city, the air here was country air. In the city he could smell the neighbours' lives all around him: what they ate, what they washed with and their cabbage breath when they awoke in the morning. Here, the air was heavy with the scent of fruity blossoms and the smells of the red, red earth as the heat was released from the soil as the air cooled.

Alphonse breathed deeply. He felt like sitting in the back yard and looking up at the stars but he had not gone out there since the night his mother had begun to foresee her death. He had done nothing to protect her memory as she would have wanted him to. He felt lost and unhappy, as if the world would never be right again.

He sat in the kitchen and stared at the oversized wooden spoon and fork which were hanging side by side on the wall. He listened for the sounds of owls but what he heard was the sound of human feet on the stones leading to the house. Alphonse did not dare to look and see who was coming.

The knock at the door was soft but urgent and Alphonse heard his name being called in a low whisper. *"Ouvré pot la."*

Alphonse did not move.

It was Delphi. *"M'ap suplié ou. Tanpri, ouvré pòt la."*

Still Alphonse did not move. He wanted Delphi to go away. *Notre Pére, qui est aux cieux.*

"Alphonse!" Delphi had walked around the house and was standing in the back yard by the chair where his mother had sat all through the night. "Alphonse! *Vin ici pou nou kab palé.*"

Alphonse stared through the darkness and saw Delphi's striped shirt. *Que ton nom soit béni. Que ton règne vienne.* It looked green and purple in the moonlight. It was ripped at the neck and pulled out from his khaki shorts. Alphonse did not want to think about what could have happened. *Que ta volonté soi faite sur terre comme au ciel.* He crossed his arms across his chest and closed his eyes. *Donne nous aujourd'hui notre pain de ce jour.*

"Alphonse. Let me in. I beg of you. Open your door." Delphi's voice was coming closer and closer to the back door.

Alphonse had left the back door open but the screen door was locked. Delphi would disappear sooner or later. What was he? A man? A spirit? It did not matter. Alphonse did not want to deal with either. *Pardonne nous nos offenses.*

Delphi's voice was rising steadily with frustration. "You don't see me? You don't hear me?" Alphonse heard the hinges of the screen door rattle. *Comme nous pardonnons aussi à ceux qui nous ont offensé.* "You don't want to know that they are after me?" Delphi laughed nervously. "They could be after you one day and who will you go to? Tell me, Alphonse. Who?"

The sounds of his mother's pigs came from the back of the yard. Alphonse had missed their usual feeding time with the visit to Mlle. Dominique's house. He felt the skin of his forehead tighten. *Et ne nous soumait pas à la tentation.*

Delphi's voice grew loud and sharp, like a rooster announcing the rising sun. "Help me. Alphonse. Help me. They have guns. I have nothing but books and words. I cannot fight them. Please, Alphi. Help your brother."

The muscles in Alphonse's back tightened and his hands closed around the muscles of his arms as if he were trying to staunch a bleeding wound. *Mais délivre nous du mal.* He heard his voice flow from his mouth, but the words were his mother's, empty, full of spite. "Why don't you run," he said flatly. "You still have feet for running, don't you?" *Ainsi soit'il.* His eyes were still closed when he heard the sound of Delphi's feet backing away from the door, like the sound of a stray after scraps of food being driven away from the kitchen. At first the steps were mincing, unbelieving, quiet. Then they were quick, lifting pebbles that skipped noisily in the quiet of the night, as if they were falling into a deep and empty well.

In the morning, Eric came knocking at the door. Alphonse had fallen asleep in his chair. He rose to open the door. "Cousin Eric," he said. "*Koman ou yé?*"

Eric had his hands on his hips, above the heavy black leather belt on which his gun was hanging in a shabby holster. He was wearing the blue shirt of the *Macoutes.* It had been pressed recently and still showed the sharp lines of a hot iron along the short sleeves. "*Sa va. Sa va,*" Eric nodded. He had an odd smile, friendly and hostile at the same time. "*Sak passé.* Don't I get to come in?"

Alphonse stood aside as Eric pushed past him into the kitchen to rummage through the cupboards. "It's already been a long morning for me. We had to go up North to stop a demonstration. You should have seen how surprised they were. I tell you, there were hundreds of them and just ten of us. They were scared! Just amazing. I shot my gun in the air and they split apart like fraying yarn. Imagine. Just one gunshot and they lost all their convictions. We had a tough time with one of them. Delphi Dominique. You know him?" Eric found a plate of fried plantain and brought it out to eat at the table. He put his feet up against another chair and looked at Alphonse. "Did you ever know him? You know, the *mambo's* son. D.D.? We've had a hard time finding him, you know. We thought he had gone back to the continent. But he came back to his mother's voice." Eric laughed. "To the mother land." He stopped to eat a handful of the plantains. "We killed him. It was very easy. He didn't even turn to run, you know! Just stared at us as if we wouldn't do it."

Alphonse stood and looked at Eric through half-closed eyes. A vein began to throb above the bridge of his nose. He knew that one day Delphi's ghost would come to find him and when that day came he would have to run, and run, and run.

CHAPTER THREE

A lizard lay beneath the table, its body bright green against the pink tiles. A bump protruded from its forehead. Its skin seemed dry as talc. Its claws clicked as it scuttled in the shadows, its thin tail sweeping small rounds of dust, while its eyes, oval and dark like watermelon seeds, closed and opened quietly.

Alphonse watched the lizard's body move up and down. It reminded him of doing press-ups in his room, the smell of the compacted dirt – stained with years of his sweat – filling his nostrils. He remembered the loneliness of working on his body for no reason but to feel the muscles straining to attention, letting him know he was still alive, that something might still be within reach. That room had absorbed his childhood, the walls closing in, the ceiling pressing him down onto his hands. He'd pushed up against it to keep from being flattened. The lizard's right eye rolled in its socket. It stepped forward, green claw hesitating, suspended in the air. Alphonse stared at the lithe fingers of the claw, each distinct, small bones encased in plastic flesh. The lizard placed the claw down on the tile. Staccato clicketing. Alphonse watched the little tail swagger from left to right as it disappeared behind the hanging tablecloth which fluttered up and down each time the door opened.

"If you see any lizards," Bella said, "Be sure you chase them out."

Alphonse nodded, not looking up at her wide, round face, her sad brown eyes. If he looked he would be sucked into her melancholy. He had known this woman almost all of his life. She seemed so unlike any of the women who had mothered him. Bella, childless and in need of comfort. Bella, so in need of mothering herself. He could not give her that. Did not want to give a love which could not be measured.

Bella sucked her teeth. "We don't want anything to go wrong. Not today."

Alphonse listened to her soft steps walking away carefully, as if she was afraid of tripping on something unexpected or placed there to make a misery of her days. He looked beneath the table and could not find the lizard. It had disappeared. He sighed, stared at the food on the table, biting his nails which were already gnawed down to the flesh.

At that moment, M'sieur Léo came down the stairs, brushing away lint from his dark suit with a manicured hand. His gold rings glittered in the half-light. His bald head gleamed like a full moon in a dark sky. Alphonse dropped his hand to his side, pushed his feet down into the soles of his shoes to ready himself for the inspection which was soon to follow.

M'sieur Léo stared him up and down. "Your job is to make sure everyone's plate is full and that they have a glass in their hand. You can do that, can't you?"

"Yes."

"Yes what?"

"Yes, I can do that." Alphonse refused to call his father sir as he wanted. There was a line to draw between servility and impassivity. He knew he would be rid of this life some day soon. He'd saved over half of his monthly allowance – a measly fifty Haitian dollars – for that purpose. He would be rid of this man, this monster who'd turned his life to dung.

M'sieur Léo's eyes shot arrows of spite towards him but Alphonse did not look away. But when he put both hands on his son's shoulders, a shudder ran through Alphonse's entire body. One day he would do something so terrible he would never be the same. One day he would kill this man.

"Bon. O.K. We understand each other." M'sieur Léo squeezed his shoulders. Bone crushing pressure. "Just don't do anything to embarrass me."

Alphonse smiled. "Of course not, M'sieur Léo." The man was a heap of garbage. Was it not his grandmother they were burying? Was it not a hard day for him too? Alphonse's smile kept back the

110

bile of anger rising into his mouth from the back of his throat. "I will do my job. As always."

M'sieur Léo squeezed his shoulders again, nodding: "Good. Good. That is all I ask."

Alphonse stood in the oval passageway leading to the dining room, outside the room where his grandmother lay. He linked his hands behind him, pushed out his chest like a shield and closed his eyes against the sight of his father bending over the table of food Bella had prepared for the guests. He could smell all the good things Bella had made: grape leaves soaked in brine wrapped around sweet tomato rice; spears of asparagus rolled in thin slices of ham; cubes of *grillot*; long-grained white rice set next to a steaming bowl of red kidney bean sauce; olives stuffed with crab; a shrimp bisque surrounded by slices of lemon; a duck glazed with an orange sauce; chicken thighs soaking in stewed hot-peppers; a Russian salad of potatoes, carrots, peas, white tuna, red beets; a *rôti* of beef carved into slices, flesh blood-pink; melting rounds of *brie* and *Camembert* with clusters of green grapes between them; rum cake crowned with a dripping sugar icing. It was all too much.

Alphonse turned his back on the table, on his father, and looked into the living room. Chairs had been arranged in a half circle around the coffin where his grandmother lay like a piece of driftwood. Yes, she had drifted away from him. He wondered how, and why. He cherished the love she had given him in morsels, over time, like the oranges she would give him when he set off back home from his days in the country with her. He would plunge the crescents of orange greedily into his mouth, always thinking that eating them in this way, hurriedly, would bring back the feeling of being in her house. But nothing made the walls of his father's cellar expand or move the ceiling higher. He ate orange after orange and made his stomach upset with the sour juices as he sat on his bed, listening in the quiet of the night to the snakes slithering by; the red rats running past his door like good neighbours; his father's footsteps falling just above his head as he walked through the rooms of the house like a man so afraid of his wealth he had to count his money every night before he went to sleep.

It would be a few hours before the dining room filled with all those people he hated, his father's business friends who came to all the christenings and funerals as if they were the proper place to close deals, exchange tips on the market or talk politics. The men drank too much, were always loud. The women, their mistresses or wives, were always self-effacing – and drank too much. The smell of alcohol would spread through the house in minutes and it would take days for it to go away, days for the scent of the sea to return. He felt sorry for his grandmother having to be surrounded by people she did not know for her last night above the earth.

M'sieur Léo's wife was sitting on a rococo couch with spindly legs and hard cushions, a glass of water in her hand. Alphonse had never seen her so calm.

"*Madanm*," he said. "*Ou bezwen kèk bagay?*"

"*Non, Alphonse.*" She cocked her head to the side and looked at him. Her eyes were a clear, transparent brown. She attempted a smile. Her mouth quivered then fell. She brought the glass of water to her lips and sipped it quietly, still watching Alphonse, the man-boy, the bastard, who had been brought into her house and ignored all these years, except when she needed an ear to talk to, a face to touch. "*Tout va bien.*"

Alphonse nodded. He could not tell if she wanted to say more.

He sensed the fabric of his suit against his skin and recalled that his grandmother had bought it some years ago when she thought he was finally going to get the chance to go to high school. This was the first time he'd had the chance to wear it. It still fitted snugly. Alphonse pulled at the cuffs, straightened himself and the back of the jacket fell softly along his spine. He thought how proud Grandmother had looked when he'd opened the box and seen the navy blue suit lying beneath the white wrapping paper. Her face, her eyes, her smile, all bright like stars. He had wanted to cry into the stiff fabric as she patted him on the back. He had been so very tired that day, working through the morning helping Bella cut wood for his father's house, for the cool nights they always had in the hills. So very tired. He'd wanted to ask his grandmother why she'd never taken him in, rather than leaving him with M'sieur Léo, her wayward son.

He remembered the weekends spent at her house in the summers, with his cousin and Désirée, the long days of doing nothing except laughing and eating. He remembered the love flowing between the girls, the grandmother and him, but always being afraid that they would shut him out. And feeling self-conscious about his clothes which were either very old, out of date or shabby, work clothes picked out by M'sieur' Léo's wife to match everyone else's who toiled in the house. He had always been afraid of saying the wrong thing, of not being courteous enough, of not being liked. Sometimes, he could tell, they forgot he was there and it would be his fault. He was so quiet. He would be sad until Grandmother would seek him out, place a hand on his head and say: "Come, we are waiting for you. You cannot hide from us."

He remembered one weekend in particular. It was Josèphe's birthday on the Sunday. She was going to be five. He was nine and, although he knew that she did not know that they were cousins, he had insisted on helping Grandmother make *crême de pistaches*. He spent an hour in the kitchen on Saturday morning crushing the peanuts in a pestle until they were fine, fine, like pieces of sand. He watched Grandmother beat the eggs and cream and other ingredients into a thick and lovely white cream. She let him fold the peanut sand into the mixture until it was blended into the shape of clouds, bumpy and light all at once. Then they had slipped the cream into a plastic bowl, shut it tightly with a lid, and placed it in the freezer overnight.

The next day, he had been filled with happiness. He helped decorate the house. He watched Josèphe follow Désirée from room to room, taping balloons low against the wall because she could not reach very high and giggling when they stuck to her hair with static. For once he did not mind the girls' closeness. He thought only of how much she would like the ice cream, how special it was that he had made it for her with his grandmother. She had smiled at him all day long until the children from the city started to come through the door smelling of expensive soaps and heavy perfumes. The girls wore pinafores in wild, bright colours with bows in their hair and gold bracelets on their wrists. The boys wore long pants with pleats that started at the waist and came down in a straight line the length of their legs. They all wore shiny leather shoes with gold or silver buckles. Alphonse had seen Désirée and Josèphe in such clothes before but it was another thing to see a cluster of children so richly attired. It made him feel small and not belonging. The boys laughed at his khaki shorts, the T-shirt that was so small it had begun to roll around his armpits. The girls called him ugly and laughed at his ears. "*Ou sé makak*," they said, running away from him and pretending to be monkeys when he tried to touch their hands and reassure them.

After an hour or so of watching the children play their games of marbles and skip-rope, Alphonse felt that he was back in his father's house, without a place. He did the only thing he knew to do: he took out the cake and lit the candles. He watched Josèphe's face light up in the candlelight before she blew the candles out. He parcelled out pieces of cake onto the plates the children impatiently handed him. He did not want to bring out the ice cream, but when he looked up he saw his grandmother opening the bowl and setting it on the table with a serving spoon. Another line formed and he stood before it, parcelling out the round balls of cream. His heart thumped in his chest. He gave Josèphe two scoops and waited to see if she would like it. She brought a tiny amount to her pursed lips and grimaced. "A-RRrr," she said as if the ice-cream was burning her throat. "*C'est pas bon du tout.*"

"*Allons. Allons,*" Grandmother said, her arm wrapped around the top of Alphonse's chest. "*Il faut essayer.* Try."

Josèphe tried again and scrunched her face against the taste of the ice cream. "It's like dirt," she said. She squealed, "Dirt ice-cream!"

Then all the children were singing out "Dirt ice-cream, Dirt ice-cream!" and Alphonse's ears were stinging. He wriggled out of his grandmother's arms, who tried to hold him and told him not to listen. Why had she invited them? Why had she let them humiliate him? Why couldn't it have been just the four of them, alone? Alphonse ran to the back of the house and climbed into the cradling branches of a blooming *quenêpier*. He longed to find himself a home, longed to be far away from here. He closed his eyes and listened to the noises of the small things in the grass he could not see. And as the bright sunlit afternoon turned dark with dusk, he cried long, quiet tears into the still night air.

Thinking back to that afternoon, Alphonse could not remember when else he had cried so hard in that childish and self-absorbed way that seemed always to follow betrayal. He had never asked why Grandmother had not come to seek him out in the darkness. He had stayed hidden up in the nest of the tree's branches for long hours waiting for her to appear, to see her hand reaching up to him, inviting him to come down. But she had never come.

He thought of the moment he realized she would not appear as he watched the stream of strangers entering the dining room to peer into his grandmother's casket. Most were still holding their drinks as they did so, and Alphonse feared that some careless person would empty his or her rum-and-Coke onto his grandmother's favourite creamy-white silk blouse. But it was not his job to keep them at a distance, to tell them to leave their food and drink in the next room before they entered here, so he stayed where he was, between the door and the casket, making sure that people were happy with the food on their plates, happy with the selection of things to drink.

There were few familiar faces. Of course, Josèphe and Désirée – who should have been there – were elsewhere. Jo had grown up far away from him. Deep inside, he still loved her – the sister he never had. He was hardly ever in contact with her. He wrote her once after his mother died, but the answer he received was in someone else's voice, not the Josèphe he had thought he knew.

Alphonse shrugged his shoulders absent-mindedly. Well, he thought, perhaps that *had* been her. The same spoiled child he had known, unwilling to extend any compassionate emotion. Still, he could not bring himself to dislike her, to find fault with her.

Désirée was another story. He had seen her often over the years and theirs had grown into an uncomfortable relationship which kept them at a distance. She would speak to him of everything she was going to do to change Haiti, of how wonderful life would be when she and her friends made everything all right. He spent days wondering what she was talking about as she sat in the yard and lounged, never asking if he needed help peeling the vegetables or watering down the uneven slabs of the porch to make them gleam in the sunlight. "Oh," she would say, as he chopped cucumber, "how delightful. I've been waiting days and days for a cucumber salad." Why didn't she make one then? Or, she would look at the water tumbling out of the hose onto the white slabs and exclaim: "What a waste of water! We could grown ten more trees with that." Then why didn't she plant some? And why did she wait for her boyfriend Charles to come to fetch her before she walked out into the streets to proclaim freedom for all? He would listen to her plans and nod and nod, always ending their conversations by saying: "Yes, it will be a great day when the people are free," cutting her with his eyes.

He did not know what had happened when he'd woken just a few days ago to hear M'sieur Léo's voice ranting about Désirée to the lady of the house.

"What does she think she's doing?"

"Calm down," *Madanm* said. "You'll disturb the boy."

"What do I care about him!"

"Come now. Calm. . ."

"Don't tell me what to do!"

Alphonse heard the familiar sound of his father's wide hand falling hard against moist and supple skin to bruise it, a sound like a fish slapped against the cutting board to be gutted. *Madanm* never cried. He could not imagine her wriggling like those freshly caught fish he had seen at the market flopping against each other wildly. *Madanm* was a defeated woman. They were alike in many ways, except that within him there was always that smouldering wick of a hope that within her had been extinguished long ago.

His father kept on at her, on and on, all morning long, repeating over and over again as he beat her into a mess of bruises the colour of currants: "What a disgrace! What a disgrace!" The words made Alphonse's stomach churn with disgust.

He remembered those words as he saw his father leading a business acquaintance down the long table of food, Alphonse's stomach had the same impulse to jump through his body and out of his mouth. The whole scene sickened him. His mind was made up. M'sieur's house was not his home, had never been.

When all the guests had left, he looked into the casket to say a last goodbye to his grandmother. Her face was stiff like wax, a lifeless brown. There was nothing left to say or do. His grand-mother's spirit had long departed for *Ginen*, to reach the ances-tors.

Tomorrow, he would buy a one-way ticket to New York and fly away from Haiti, old pearl of the Antillean Sea. He would forget the disappointment, the anger, the pain. America would gather him up in her strong arms and cradle him gently to sleep.

Yes, America. Yes. Tomorrow, he would go.

CHAPTER FOUR

I, Alphonse, give and dedicate my self and my life to our Saviour Jesus Christ, my actions, pains and sufferings, to use no part of my being except to honour, love, and glorify him.

Leaving the island behind was not as he had imagined. As the plane soared high above the mountains and out over the sea, Alphonse felt his chest close in on itself, his heart sink into the pit of his stomach. He clutched the armrests, plush and blue, with both hands. He did not let go until they were far into the sky and he could see only layer upon layer of rain clouds rimmed with grey and turquoise. Often, he caught himself holding his breath, fearful that the whir of the engine would suddenly stop and the plane would tumble out of the sky. He immediately missed everything he had left behind – even those things which were no longer there to return to. As the island became a small, green-brown olive below him, memories of his mother, of the small room below the monstrous house which had held him captive for so long, of his grandmother in her casket and the closed face of his father as he had handed him money and instructions on how to get by in the Big City: all these drew him back. But he was free now, was he not? Free as a bird.

When Alphonse stepped out from the plane to walk down the long corridor lined with pictures of places even farther away, like Paris and Munich, he thought he could smell America as one smells a new and exotic fruit. Clean, he thought. There was a smell of clean like nothing he had ever known before. Not like the smell of sea water and the pungent buds of flowers but the smell of squeaky plastic, new jeans, crisp dollar bills. The air was heavy, humid with the promise of rain. Alphonse could not believe he had made it as he emerged from the corridor and into the bright fluorescent lights of the terminal.

A thrill went through his body. The terminal was crowded with all kinds of people, on their way to or from places he could only dream of seeing one day. He felt strangely alive, as if he had just risen from his sick-bed and was walking his first tentative steps after days of lying in the stench of his own sweat. The bustling crowds reminded him of the *lakou-foumi* in Port-au-Prince – the market place, the squares. He could see fragments of the people he knew in each of the faces that sped past him. The only difference he could see was that those who looked alike walked together, in small, protective clumps.

Alphonse meandered through the clusters, taking his time. He had nowhere to be and his heart was beating fast. His hands grew sticky around the handle of the cracked leather bag which held his meagre belongings; a few shirts, pants, a good pair of shoes, socks, and a selection of his sports' magazines. His feet seemed unnaturally large and clumsy as he bumped into a soft and plump body and had to excuse himself. *Louk wear yu goin'*. Strange tongues flew towards him and he smiled in answer, not knowing what else to do.

He was standing in a store promising to give him a piece of America of his very own when he noticed a man next to him who was touching everything in sight with shaking hands. The man was young, maybe his own age, with long sideburns and a headful of shaggy, dirty-blonde hair. The man was looking at everyone out of the corner of his eyes. Alphonse feigned interest in a small statuette of the Statue of Liberty carved out of green marble. The man moved away from him and Alphonse noticed that there were two of them in the store walking jerkily in a half-circle around the stands of T-shirts and ceramic apples with bites taken out of them. Ballpoint pens with moving ships sliding down the handles found their way into their pockets. Rolled magazines followed, then earrings made of silver and small stones, then bars of chocolate and shot glasses rimmed with gold. Could this be America?

The raised hand of Ms. Liberty dug into Alphonse's palm as he watched the men make their way out of this store and into the next. He watched as two large men with walkie-talkies came running out of the crowd, shirt-tails flying against faded jeans. They pulled the two young men by the collars of their jackets and threw them to the ground, screaming: *Faught yu woz goin' to gt awé wit it, é! Faught yu woz goin' to gt awé frum uss!* The large men seemed exhilarated as they punched the bodies of the thieves and locked their hands behind their backs in silver handcuffs. Alphonse shuddered, remembering the sight of Macoutes doing the same at home, but with much more violence, so much blood flowing. He began to think that they would come after him next when he caught the eye of one of the heavy-set men whose face had turned beet pink. Alphonse turned away. He knew he looked like someone who had done something wrong. He did not want to be mistaken for an accomplice. He did not know what to do.

"*Ou vlé bagay sa-a?*"

Alphonse turned around to see where the voice was coming from. It was coming from behind a cash register covered with decals of credit card logos.

"Would you like to make a purchase?" The voice was soft, soothing, so quiet and of home. Mami.

Alphonse looked into the face belonging to the voice which made him want to return to Haiti. He stepped back. It was his brother Delphi looking back at him, eyes round, milky with disappointment, the haughty eyebrows flying up into his forehead. Alphonse dropped the statue and heard it break when it hit the ground, the pieces flying across the glossy tile floor. He was still holding his bag in his other hand, holding it fiercely.

"M'sieur," he heard, "M'sieur?"

And then there were the feet of the big, lumbering men and the jiggling of the keys on their wide, black leather belts: *Wi gat anuver won, boiz. Wer yu fink yu goin', sun?*

Alphonse ran out of the terminal and banged on the side of a bus which was pulling away from the curb with his fists. The doors closed behind his back just in time. He was beginning his first month of America in fine style.

It is now my irrevocable will to be completely His and to do all for

120

His love, by renouncing with all my heart all that could displease Him.

Weeks later he was still thinking about that face behind the counter. It followed him into his dreams like a vapour, the scent of a faraway time when he had been sure of himself, of the thin distance between right and wrong. Delphi. It was ten years ago now, killed by the Macoutes because of Alphonse's need to be true to his mother's folly. Delphi had followed him into the heart of America like a parasitic worm!

Alphonse lay back on the bed in the apartment he had rented a few days after arriving at the airport with the same name as the street on which Delphi had been killed: J.F.K.. M'sieur Léo had given him the name of one of his business contacts, a Mr. Guillaume. The man had been easy to find at the end of a telephone line in Manhattan. Mr. Guillaume had given him a one-room apartment for two hundred and fifty dollars a month. Alphonse thought it had been as a favour to his father, but now he knew why it was so cheap. With his eyes closed he could hear the cockroaches zigzagging across the linoleum floor of the kitchen and up the chipped whitewashed wall behind his head. The noise of their hundreds of feet reminded him of the lizard at his grandmother's wake. They made his skin crawl.

The day after he had moved into the apartment he had gone to the stove to boil some water and found a rust-red cockroach swimming in water he had left standing overnight. The pests here were like nothing he had seen before. They did not know their place. Scavengers of the worse kind. At least he was not out on the street. For that, he was thankful. He had made it to the second month of America.

I take you, then, O Sacred Heart, as the only object of my love, protector of my life, assurer of my faith, remedy to my fragility and inconsistency, repairer of all the faults of my life, my sure safe harbour at the hour of my death.

In the third month of his coming to America, Alphonse decided to go back to the J.F.K. airport to see if his nightmares were real.

He wanted to see again the woman with the face of Delphi. Delphi in a woman's face.

And there she was, as he came into the Piece-of-Americana store, smiling at him as if she had been waiting all these weeks for him to return. As if they already knew each other.

"*Kòman ou yé, cheri?*"

She was like a sister in this foreign place. Someone to hold on to when he missed Port-au-Prince and missed seeing the women walk past his mother's house on their way to the *marché*. He had thought he would never see such women again. He was mesmerized by her hair, a pleat several inches thick wrapped around her head like a weaving of sweet grass. He wanted to reach over the glass counter and undo the crisscrossing strands, run his fingers through its thick softness to touch the scalp and feel the oils tying them together, as if in ceremony.

The woman spoke again. "*Kòman ou yé?*"

The depth of her voice made him think of a dense forest, forced him to look into her eyes. So soft, so full of love for one she did not know. How could she look at him with those eyes? Delphi's eyes. How did Delphi find his way into her lovely, forest-dark face?

Alphonse smiled at her, feeling all his energies drain from his body. He could not speak to her and betray himself. If he spoke, he would have to speak to Delphi's ghost and he was not ready for that, not ready to be forgiven. Instead, he slid his last ten dollar bill towards her on the counter to pay for the statuette he had broken. He left the store sure he would never return.

Be then, O Beatific Heart, my justification before God the Father, turn away from me the marks of His just anger.

Alphonse found the Lord in the fifth month of America.

The Lord spoke to him in hushed tones as he rushed from one job interview to the next and was turned away. Men with fat bellies, shirts popping open around their navels, yelped at him from across their metal desks: *Wair yu lern tu speke anglich, boi? Wat yu gut ver ina yur mouf? Spekaup, boi. Dnt vé tich ya howa tu speka anglish don ver ina Tahiti?* He tried to make sense of their words, tried to imitate their sounds, but they laughed at him, laughed at the way the words came out sounding strange and misshapen, like lumps of heavy dough falling from his lips. He felt strange and misshapen each time he exited the back room office of a diner or junk shop with another business card smeared with oily fingerprints. He was qualified for nothing except being a servant. And here, in America, they preferred women, round and plump. He did not know if there were truly such women, but he saw them on boxes in the super-market, beaming happiness over pictures of waffles and corn syrup. Alphonse was tall and thin and quiet. He could do as he was told, but he could not smile all day long at people who hated him. He could not. He would not.

The Lord says: Pray onto me and your life will have meaning. Pray onto me and the world around you will be beatific, yours to navigate, possess.

Alphonse was not sure if it really was the Lord speaking to him, but he saw the face of the Magnificent One in his dreams. The One floated through space towards him, alongside the woman with Delphi's eyes. There was a struggle going on inside him but Alphonse could not grasp its horns, wrestle it to the ground and vanquish it. He did not know if he was more afraid of Delphi or of the Lord. They had the same eyes: full of sorrow, pain – disappointment in him.

O Heart of Love, I place all my faith in You, for I have all to fear of my malice and my weakness, but I have all to hope from Your goodness.

Alphonse found a job stocking shelves and sweeping the floor in a drugstore. He made less than three dollars an hour because he could not produce a green card the day the man gave him the job – by handing him a smock and waving him down the aisles. Now he could pay his rent, be free of his father's beneficence. He could go to the bars and stand against the counter with the confidence that he would be able to pay for at least one drink of hard liquor. Yet Alphonse still felt something was eating away at him. Every time he brought a drink to his lips he could see the bartender looking at him with those same – Delphi's – soulful eyes. It made the drinks burn the back of his throat and his head hurt even before the alcohol had time to flow into his veins, into his brain.

Alphonse walked out of the bar in this, his sixth month of America, with one of the women he had once feared, with rouged lips and easy laughter, falling against his arm. He knew her from another time. She raised a hand towards him after he had sat down at the bar and asked him to join her at a table at the back of the room. She sat below the faded poster of a street lined with coconut trees they all pretended was a street from home.

"*Frè*," she said, "*Kòman ou yé?*"

Alphonse's heart began to thump and he smiled at her, nodding.

"I have been watching you," she said. "You are new to New York, aren't you? So am I. Well, maybe not so new. Two years, I have been here. Two years too long." She sighed and put a hand on his arm and Alphonse felt such warmth coursing through her fingers and into his skin. He wanted to pull away but did not want to offend her. He looked into her face. Her eyes were the shape of almonds, slightly bulbous. Her eyebrows were plucked and looked like the wings of sea gulls when they hover far away in the distance. Her lips were red, red and outlined in purple-brown. He could not see her hair; it was hidden beneath a blue headdress. She had a gold necklace around her neck with a pendant in the shape of a cross balancing between her breasts. "You should not stay here," she continued. "You do not belong here. Go back before it is too late."

Alphonse smiled, shrugged, was happy that Delphi was not in her eyes, judging him. He bought her drink after drink and she talked and talked about her life working as a counsellor to teenage girls in Brooklyn, how she would like to return to her home in Jacmel and do something for her people. He just sat and listened until she said to him: "I like you." And then, "I want you to take me home." All Alphonse could think of was of taking her to meet his mother, but he could only take her to his rented room. His heart sank at the thought of the skittering cockroaches, but he nodded yes. He could try to do this – the strange ritual of all the

124

men in the bar – of taking a woman home you didn't really know or want to know, sleeping with her, making her leave in the morning, and then coming to the bar the next day and ignoring her when she called out your name in heated expectation.

Consume in me, then, all which may displease or resist You. May Your pure love impress itself so deeply within my heart that I may never forget nor be separated from You. And through Your will my name shall be written in You since I want all of my happiness and glory to consist of living and dying in enslavement to You.

They wandered slowly down the street in the general direction of his apartment building, but Alphonse could not stand the thought of having to bring the woman into its smells of urine and garbage and up the elevator so old it could only carry three people uncomfortably, so he took her instead a block further, to a residential hotel run by Catholic priests who no longer wore the cassock, but walked around in plain clothes as if they were ordinary people. There the rooms would be small, but the beds would be made, and the wash basins would be white as first snow, ready to be filled with water to wash away their uncleanliness. They stumbled into the lobby of the hotel and Alphonse signed them in as Monsieur et Madame next to the date: November 1991. He smiled at the hotel clerk and there it was again. Those eyes. Large. Round. Mocking him. The eyes were looking past him at the woman and Alphonse turned to face her. She was younger than he thought when he first saw her at the bar, smoking a cigarette in the corner. She was wearing a simple dress which accentuated the curves of her body, though those curves were slight. She could not have been any older than his cousin Josèphe was now – early twenties, barely. *The Lord whispers: Pray unto me.* Alphonse smiled at the girl and tried to ignore the man behind the counter with Delphi's eyes. He handed the clerk thirty dollars and walked ahead of the girl, guiding her up the stairs, holding her hand, which was so small in his it felt like holding a little bird.

In the room, he held her in his arms before turning on the light. Her back was against the door and Alphonse took in the smell of smoke in her hair. But he could also smell a faraway hint of coconut milk and mango. He buried his face in the tight curls and imagined her standing in a bathtub early that morning, before her thoughts had brought her to the bar. The water would have cascaded down her body, forming rivers along the smooth brown of her neck, meandering over breasts the shape of red-green mangoes grown ripe, as she held her arms high above her head and twisted her hair into a coil around her fingers. Her body would have purified the water as it dribbled down towards her navel and filled it, as if it were a small, hollow piece of parched earth, then spilled over her thighs before it splashed against her feet like raindrops.

When he finally released her from his arms to turn on the light he saw that she had been crying. There were pools of black beneath her eyes and black half-circles staining the collar of his shirt. He placed his hands on her shoulders.

"*Sa pa-p fè anyen,*" he said. "Go wash your face and you can go to sleep."

Her face was full of surprise, lit up like a rainbow, as if he had given her an unexpected gift.

Alphonse's heart puffed with compassion. He smiled as she walked to the bathroom and shut the door behind her gingerly.

He was left sitting on the bed looking up at the bathroom door. He opened the drawer of the night stand and took out the Bible he knew he would find there. A card fell out of the pages and he saw it was a picture of the Lord with Delphi's eyes reaching out to him, rays of sunlight shooting out from thin, delicate fingers. Alphonse closed his eyes. When he opened them, the picture on the card had changed into a drawing of the Sacred Heart, thorns digging into the red flesh. Alphonse's hands trembled as he held the card. On the back was the prayer he had been reciting every first Friday of the month to gain a pardon from the Lord for failing to protect his brother from the men in blue, to gain a seat in heaven. It was printed in blue, scripted letters. He knew now he would never come to the end of the required nine months. He did not have the faith, the blinding hope.

The girl emerged from the bathroom wrapped in a towel, hair flat with water and took the card from his hands. "Oh," she said.

126

"It's a hologram. See." She moved the card back and forth in the light. "Two pictures instead of one." She handed him back the card but Alphonse could only see one picture: the eyes of Delphi and the Lord overlapping atop the Sacred Heart and felt the clarity of his betrayal of them both.

He lay down beside the warm body of the girl after she had wriggled beneath the sheets and fallen asleep. He watched her eyes flutter beneath her eyelids and would have liked to see her dreams. Her soft features reminded him again of his young cousin, so vulnerable, so closed in upon herself the last time he saw her on her last trip back to Haiti, years ago. He would have to begin again here, with this woman. He would not harm her in any way. He touched the girl's face and her cheek twitched like the body of a small, wounded bird whose wings had been broken and could not fly. His heart bloomed like a rose opening against the morning dew – blood red petals of pain, widening, widening, finally unafraid of admitting thorns.

MAMI CÉLESTE
(1400-1492/1784-1800
1934-1976/1979-1991)

"Even though I walk through the
valley of the shadow of death, I fear no evil."
Psalms 23:4

The ocean is a deep and unforgettable blue, clear and clean like some oasis put aside for the gods. The hills, blanketed with a dense forest of fir trees, stand tall and majestic surveying the waters like tireless sentinels. The narrow trails leading away from the white foamy beaches disappear rapidly into the mysteries of the interior. The mysterious isle. The secret isle. The land of forgetting and new awakenings. These are some of the words the invaders will use to describe the jutting slabs of mossy earth which seem to have come from nowhere to interrupt their voyage to find spices and gold. But here is something not at all expected, they will think, here is something God has placed in our path so that we may take from it what is there to take. They will not notice the hidden trails, the billows of smoke rising from the duvet of tall firs, the hollowed-out shells of tree trunks left blanching on the shore where they will drop their heavy anchors. No, they will rush onto this hallowed ground and kiss the sandy beach, letting the grains hang on their dewy lips, the hairs on their chests. They will rush onto that land and throw their arms up to the sky and yell GRACIAS! to their great Lord above as they throw the flag of the Spanish King onto this paradise playground. Then they will play.

They will play like children with the waves of the sea they had cursed during their voyage, now a toy for their amusement as they wade in and out of the water, drawing zigzags on the sand. They will play at climbing the coconut trees to reach the larger-than-life orange orbs above, wearing their flimsy shirts tied about their heads to protect them from the sun. They will play at naming the island – finally settling on "Hispaniola" after the great fatherland. How could they have done otherwise?

But when they find that they are not alone, that others want to join in their play and show them other games, they will grow sullen and bitter with selfishness. Like children, they will want to hold onto the image of the playground as theirs and only theirs. It was God who put this jewel in their hands and they will defend it to the death. They name the interlopers (because isn't that what they are, these interlopers on the land given by the Lord to the Crown of Spain) "Indians" after the place they had not found and tell them that they have come to save them. It does not take long for the clear blue sea to discolour with the red blood spilled in the name of naming.

This is not a story. It is a memory of long, long ago when once I was alive and saw how things were then. The land looked different. The smells were different. This is not nostalgia. This is a piece of my life, etched in my brain-cells like a language. I lived, I saw. I know that I was older in the flesh than I have ever been since; my skin wrinkled about my bones, dangling like a spider's web, thin and translucent. The year the invaders came I sat in a chair made of sweet smelling plants at the top of a hill where the fir trees sheltered me from the winds flying off the ocean. I sat and watched and smiled as they frolicked and then my smile turned to stone when I realized that they were fighting the children of the people, my people. The sand turned from white to the black of blood spilled upon blood. I sat with tears refusing to spill themselves, frozen like a statue of salt. I waited for the invaders to climb the hills on their spindly legs, legs pumping with eagerness to reach the top of the hill. When they came upon me they stared at me, my wasted body; they laughed, and the last I remember is the smell of burning sweetgrass. The stink of my burning flesh.

The hills look on knowing that their fate will be worse than death as the long-haired men from far away climb their mounds and into their fissures and order the cutting down of fir trees hundreds of years old so that they can dig up the gold nuggets, the slivers of silver, the black, black coal below the roots. The hills will die a thousand deaths as they are disembowelled of their riches. And this is Hispaniola. This is the land we are left with, beautiful, violated, dying, struggling to be reborn. A place of constant metamorphosis and contradiction.

When I return to this land, it does not seem so beautiful with its scars, its mutilations exposed for all to see. When I return to this land, it is in a new body, a different body, a body which does not quite suit me. This body is young and supple and doesn't yet know of life's troubles. But it learns very quickly as I work in the fields, cutting cane. The flesh of my hands, of my feet, is sliced open over and over again; tissue grows over tissue in repair. I grow thick, unlike myself. Everyday, I battle this body and my body is embattled by the work, the scorching sun, the overseer with his whip, his gold teeth glinting at me in the night when his soft hands travel over my coarsened body in search of himself. I teach this body to know nothing, to remember nothing. I expel the tiny seeds of children I could have had, will never have; lumps of flesh and blood fall from my body like excrement. I am saddened by this body which is not mine, which cannot be made mine. I turn to the land, it teaches me patience. I become again one with its secrets, as once I was. I learn again which seeds will poison and give these to the overseer crushed in drinking water. It all seems to happen so quickly then: his death, then mine: the dragging of my body to be tied to a piece of wood, the splitting of my hardened flesh with the lash held by a hand I do not see: a final scream I do not recognize as mine yet which frees itself from my throat and rises into the sky. Songs are sung by others who are enslaved here to buoy my departing spirit.

Then there is yet another return, in a body which feels much like the first, which knows all and yet is young. The land continues to whisper to me; it is a live, huge pulsating heart. In this body, I can walk the streets freely, I can choose where I will sit and where I will stand, whom to love and whom to despise. My hands are smooth, long, filled with veins showing me that I have caught up with my past. My lives converge here, in these hands. I will live. I will love. I will make children and tend to them. I will grow every kind of plant imaginable. I will cure the sick, the lonely, the errant spirits. This is the life I have dreamed of since the day the invaders plunged onto our shores like comets.

But I am so eager to embrace this life that I marry when I am too young, barely sixteen, and I have five children, in quick succession. My husband, a young man himself, unsure of himself, is maddened by the cries of the young lives he has helped bring into the world. One day, I wake to wonder how I came to love this man. One day, there are elections and this side of the island undergoes a horrifying transformation. My husband leaves me when it seems that all the world has changed and that he too can have a little piece of the power that was once only for the invaders. I am left alone. From time to time I see him walking through the streets in a blue uniform. I do not know what he does all day long, but I know that it is nothing to be proud of. When he tries to reach out to his children in the street, I call them back to me. Always, they are angry with me, as if it was I who left them in a house too small for their needs, as if it was I who had chosen to stick a gun on my hip and call it my life. Their tears, their hunger, their anger: they will never forgive me for these crimes I have not committed.

Once, the children ran to find me in the garden. They had seen corpses, they said. For days, there had been corpses in the streets. For days, I hoped the children would not come across one of these bloating bodies, the flies buzzing in and out of their cavities. But the children walk to and from school; there is little that I can protect them from, beyond the usual cautions. If something is lying in the street – a rotting, reeking thing – there is nothing I can do to blind them. My children do not know beautiful things and I cannot teach them to look away from things which have no beauty. But the corpses do not frighten them. This is when I know that I will lose them. I know, too, that some of these bodies have had their lives snuffed out by their father and his blue comrades. The drains-water which is left to meander down the hilly streets runs pink with blood. Even the market women do not let it soak their blistering feet.

This life is not what it should be. It is not as easy as I thought it would be. The woman next door, Carmel, an older woman who is also alone, tries to help me. Her children are grown. They are mostly out of the house. It is from her that I learn of Ezili and the secrets of *voudou*. What she tells me comes in the form of memories from her childhood. Everything is hazy to her and she doesn't seem to know whether she is telling me stories or true things. I believe in all that is stored in the mind, even what appears to be untrue. What matters is that it bears the stamp of honesty.

And Carmel is an honest woman. She shows me her votive saint, her book of prayers. After speaking with her, my ears are opened to sounds I could not hear before: the pounding of drums, the soft brush of bare feet against the soil during the ceremonial dances. I see the ways in which certain lights are hung to signal that a gathering will take place. I take to following these signposts when the children are tucked in their beds and fast asleep. I spawn two lives. One is with the children and the other is cloaked in moonlight. I learn to balance night and day, moon and sun.

Carmel introduces me to women my own age. Many of these are working women like Janine. Janine has a birthmark across the bridge of her nose which makes me think of a butterfly at rest. She is a young soul. It is difficult to know what she thinks and why. She is shy and she is afraid of the dark. It is she who sits with the children when I go for walks; it allows her to keep a light on as she sews deep into the heart of the night. She is like a child herself, in need of protection. I share my life with her as Carmel has shared hers with me, providing information about things which seem beyond understanding: how to grow a plant, how to kill human beings, how to worship the sound of the rain, how to detest the men in blue without losing one's mind. But years later she will become twisted with hate, hateful.

Carmel's oldest boy, Léo, helps me from time to time with the gardening. He does not help very much. He mostly stands and watches as I turn the earth and clutch it in handfuls in my hands, letting the grains fall between my fingers. I cut the dying branches of the rose bushes; I talk to them in hushed tones to encourage them to grow. And they return my attention with new buds, heads filled with thick and veined petals of red, pink and yellow, and sturdy thorns to keep enemies at bay. Léo watches and lets me know when one of the children begins to cry. I do not realize until then that I have an enemy in the garden, so needy am I.

When a man watches and does not move to comfort a child, a child he is supposed to father, a child he is supposed to love, then you know that you are lying with an enemy. I know this when I wake in the morning and Léo is there beside me, his body hard like a fist. I do not know what has brought me here. We are not married. I thought it might be love, but it was the same lust which brought the men with long yellow hair bounding up the hills of this land in search of something sweet and pungent they could smell in the wind swirling about their heads. It was evidently nothing important for, like the first one, the one I had married, Léo soon departed. He was young and though I, too, was young, he thought I seemed so much older with my five children and a body which had turned soft and stretched, an odd round like an avocado. But there was a child he did not come to know.

This child I name Delphi. He would not be like any other child I could raise. He is not a coward like his father. He is not naive like his mother. I teach him everything I know about the land, its plants, its gifts, and yet he knows more than I can tell. It was then that I knew that this life I was living had more than one purpose; it had the quality of sunlight, bright and transparent, nurturing the soul, and it also had the quality of sunset, colourful and sombre, giving birth to something not itself. I was Delphi's sunset, bringing him into this world to tend to him as I did my flowers. And Delphi was my sunlight, a bright and beautiful thing that nothing could kill away, nurturing the soul I had carried from this world to *Ginen* and back again.

I saw Carmel less often then. I do not know what she thought of her son's departure, a grandson's birth. I never told her of my relationship with her son. To this day, no one has known but Delphi himself, and later, because it became necessary, his father. Years later there was another nameless grandson, Janine's son. He was the image of Léo, while Delphi looked more like me. We denied any resemblance, a self-deception intended to avoid shame.

Delphi grows up alongside my other children but it is clear that he is different. The others are bound to earthly pleasures and flight. They want to know their father, the man who left me behind, or their second father, the other man who left us all behind. They trample my flower-beds, they come and go as they please. They know only their own thirst, the hunger of their stomachs. Their world is limited to their bodies and nothing I can do stretches their minds. They cannot recognize beauty when they see it, not even in themselves. As soon as they are old enough, they take all that I have given them, their clothes, their bits of broken toys, the money they have made at market selling my flowers and they leave me behind, following in their fathers' footsteps. And it is Delphi who tells me not to worry, who dries my tears. *It is the way they are*, he says, and then continues, *everything is as it should be*. But even Delphi grows restless here, among the flowers, the herbal plants, with the sick and dying always at the door waiting to be handed a cure for their ailments. He wants to see the world. He feels called to be more than a gardener, a healer.

It has been years since I spoke to Léo. He is now a wealthy man, married, childless, living in the hills of Port-au-Prince in a house full of rooms empty of laughter, of love. There is no one else I can turn to in order to ensure my son's future but his father. I realize that I am a proud woman when it takes me days before I can bring myself to send word to Léo about his son's needs. The reply is short, abruptly so. Léo agrees to send Delphi away to work and study; he has connections with the U.S. armed services; it will not be a problem, even though Delphi does not carry his name. It is a painful departure, watching one so young and full of hope leaving for his travels. I still do not understand how this has come to be. It is beyond my understanding. But he will see the world, or what he needs to know of it in order to come back to this land, to hold its soil in his hands.

Not to surrender to grief, I initiate myself in one of the *voudou* cults I have come to know; I want to become a priestess of this land. I learn to give my body over to the pleasures of the gods. I learn to expect nothing from others. I learn to see those who are in need and heal their spirits as well as I know how to heal the body. They call me Mami Céleste here, just as Delphi does. I feel at home.

The blood which flows in the streets knows many victims. First it comes from the bodies which have been slain; then it flows from the hearts of those who loved the souls encased in those bodies. In the underground, there are children who have no mothers, no fathers, no kin of any sort. They do not know if they are coming or going. They have little faith, even less hope. I wonder why they come to the house until I begin to speak to them and they look to me with wide and trusting eyes. They are here because I am here and I finally understand that Delphi and I are like two sides of a coin. We have been brought to this land to serve these children, these orphans who must look up at someone with trust in their eyes, hope clutched in their hands like a rare fruit. They are my second family, my second chance. I forget my home, my flowers, to tend to them, gathering them to me at night to tell them stories. No child, I think, should not have the gift of story.

When I tell the story of Christophe falling on the shore to kiss the ground, the children look up at me with their saucer eyes and I can see that they are thinking: *How could this not be so? Of course, Christophe would have kissed his motherland.* They cannot tell the difference between Christophe Colon and Christophe, King of Haiti. In their minds they are the same person, a man in love with their homeland Haiti (and how could anyone not love this land which in all its misery still survives, still yields the same beautiful fruits and songs), a man in love with a tragic sense of the meaning of progress, a man in love with himself. I explain to them that there is a difference: Christophe Colon began the cycle of hate and self-hate, *le roi Christophe* may have kept that cycle going but he was one of us. I want them to remember something they cannot recall: that once this land was sacred and one of the most beautiful creations of all this world. They nod at me but they do not understand. I cannot teach them something which is not real, which lies somewhere above their heads in the imagination.

The lives of these children – my life – are bound up with the physical demands of rising from sleep, working to find food to eat, and hopefully making it to the time of falling back into sleep. They tell me they do not dream. They are not really children at all. So I tell them: you see, that day when the long-haired men came to this land and played on the beach as if they were children like you, they took your dreams away. What is there to dream about, they ask, if they took all the dreams away, back across the ocean to the land they came from? I cannot give back to them what never was, and so I cry the tears I could not cry in the days when my own children went from my house. Sometimes it seems to me that I can hear the hills crying with me in the whispers of the last few fir trees left. My mind begins to split into a thousand pieces of refracting glass.

During this time, Delphi sails the sea under a flag which is not his and I call out to him to return to this land which has not forsaken him. I ask him to return to these children who need his words, his knowledge, his courage. I call him for myself. When he returns I feel him again, as I knew him when he lay in my womb – such a small thing to have grown into this man – before his feet even touch the land. I do not explain to him the neglected state of the house, the overgrown weeds. I do not explain the state of my mind in all its fractured pieces. He shows me maps and talks to me of revolution, of freedom. I remember the sting of the whip, the body which was not my own splitting open like a kidney bean roasted over an open flame. I smile at him and steady myself against his arm as I look over the maps he has drawn of the mountains and the ridges and the riverbeds which I once knew as lush and overflowing with new buds of life. In the evenings, I lead him to the children; he teaches them to read and write revolution, to live and breathe freedom.

At times, the men in blue come up to the house, asking questions I will not answer: Where does Delphi work? What does he teach? Where are his textbooks? Delphi begins to disappear, first for an afternoon, then for a day, then for weeks. The pieces of glass which make up my brain show me pictures of his body lying in pools of blood, torn bits of his flesh sticking to the pavement. I am afraid during his absences. My house falls in disrepair.

There are vines growing in every direction, overrunning the pavement, climbing up the walls of the house. The flowers still stand in quiet vigil. I come to them to touch their soft new buds. They silence the disquiet in my mind, the burning behind my eyes, the vision of my son falling to the ground and being dragged away by the men in blue. I am so tired, so blind with my own grief. There must be something I can do, something to repair this throwing away of life after life, body after body. I do not know what it is. I talk aloud to myself, to the flowers, to the gods above. The neighbours stare after me, pity me – I see it in their eyes. The children who play in the streets call me names, play tricks on me. I have no time to chide them and tell them to mind their ways.

Delphi returns, time and time again, his body marked by his absences, gouged with bits of metal and fire. He grows silent,

137

stunned. His steps are slow and unsure. I feed him the roots of plants which will give him strength, ease his mind. He smiles in gratitude like the children I tell stories to.

Then there is the day of the demonstration. I leave before the sunrise to take a *tap-tap* north. It is so overcrowded that bodies are pushing themselves out of its windows. Still I climb its steps and find room for my body which seems to be shrinking with time. The ride is long and the bus is too hot, but it is like riding the freedom-train Delphi told me about, the train which took the Africans out of the American South to the North, to their liberation. I will meet the children and help them to ready themselves for the walk of peace they plan to hold in defiance of the horrors they are forced to see each day. I will wait with them for Delphi to reach us. We do not know where he is. We can only hope for his safe return.

We are beginning to march when Delphi walks up to us on the dirt road, a smile on his face. The children give him a placard and begin to follow him through the streets. And then I watch as he falls under a hail of bullets. A man his own age is standing over his body, laughing. I hear, for the second time in my life, a scream, rising from my throat. It wraps itself with the laughter, struggles to lift itself above it. The sky is blue. My son is dead. I smell the scent of sweetgrass and much, much later, in the dark cell of a prison, the smell of my own burning flesh in the interrogation rooms. The children are crying in the dark. This is the end of yet another life.

I struggle to begin again the day a bird comes to the window of the jail with a flower hanging from its beak. I recognize it as one from my garden. I take it as a sign that I must be born again, live on. But it is not so easy this time. I am still encased in this body, my mind is tortured, my spirit almost broken. The children huddle against me in the dark, their fingers groping for food I do not have. Without thinking, I do what must be done. I distil the fluids of our bodies so that we may have water to drink. I pray to Ezili. We recreate the rituals to Legba so that our jailers will throw open the doors to our destiny. But we assume that our destiny is life. We assume that freedom is our right. Were there not others here before us? Did not other bodies lie here in the sweat and dung, flies buzzing above their heads, waiting for deliverance? But they were not us and we must believe that our fates will not be the same. After a week of prayers offered in steadfast faith, a blinding light greets us one morning. It is the sunlight streaming in the room, bathing our faces like the waters from a fresh pond. The door has been opened and we are pushed out, stumbling, from the jail. There are gods watching over us.

The children I let run back to the clearing in the forest where the others will take care of their needs. I will return to my home, but this time, I will not lose myself, I will begin again. For there is much to be done.

Life in the *mornes* is much the same as it was long ago before the years of drought and famine. We are nourished by the same ripe fruits, the same rays of sun, the same shade of trees. We bathe in the same clear waters running down the hills and do our washing on the banks of the rivers which now run shallow and reveal the rounded stones of their beds. The main difference is that we can only be nourished by what is left behind after the invaders (who now include some of us) have taken their pleasure from the land, and often from our bodies as well. (They mistake us for plants they can pick casually from the ground then leave to rot.) Now we rush towards their cars with the produce which was once free for the taking and are forced to sell it, or else perish ourselves. We sell in order to buy milled grains for our meals and manufactured clothes – the necessities. All this because some of our foreparents were brought to this land in chains and it was decided then that this land could never be freely ours, that we would have to buy it back with our work and our sorrow. And this is what we have been doing all these many years, ever since the day of Independence, which came much too late. It is simple: those of us who have stayed close to the land know that it is larger than any of us. We keep alive the ways of our homelands, which so many of us have begun to forget. We resist. We subsist. We recreate ourselves in the name of the ancestors.

PART THREE

DÉSIRÉE'S STORY

CHAPTER ONE

Chère Josèphe,

There will be a day when you wake and your bones will weigh you down. You will think that it is the hours of your life catching up with you to drag you down, but it will not be the process of aging which will make you so tired. It will be the weight of your mind and the caches of memory trapped there like small animals gnawing themselves out of rusty traps. Like those small creatures, you will writhe in pain and wish that memories had never been made to haunt and torture you so. There will be a day when you will recognize that you cannot escape the acts of unkindness you have perpetrated against others and against yourself.

You will remember the days when you were young and wonder where they have gone. At first, you will be inundated with the comfortable nostalgia of what will seem to be the treasure of a precious time. You will remember yourself, small, smiling, skin soft like rose petals, eyes sparkling with mischief. Then you will remember that your eyes were mischievous for a reason. You will remember your cousins who loved you so and thought you were the most special girl in the world. You will remember that you too thought you were special. You will remember that you did not think they were so special, at least, not most of the time, that you treated Alphonse as if he was your servant, making him clean up after you, fetching things for you like a dog. You will remember his child-face, as soft and supple as your own, wondering what you were up to. You will remember

141

making him your confidant when you grew older, how you talked together of your absent parents, of your separate yet similar alienation, your abandonment. You will remember reminding him that he was not as abandoned as you, since you were legitimate and he'd always been without a name in a society where only names mattered, especially your father's name. You will remember Alphonse's face closing up against you, attempting not to betray his anger because you had dared to mock him. You will remember not caring. That you liked to be cruel.

Jo, I ask you: Was there ever a time when we were free?

There will be a time when you will wish that you could not remember. But memory is not a muscle; it is a reflex; it is as natural as breathing.

You look upon your grandmother, Carmel, and wonder what memories will flood her in the last moments before she dies. But no one will ever be able to tell you what occurs at the moment of death. What is this death but something we have invented to fit our needs, a word for finality, a word for the end that we never know until we meet it and have no choice but to embrace? You look at Carmel and wonder what her memories of you are like. When she passes, will she remember the child you once were, innocent, at times indifferent, even wicked? Will she remember the girl she found going through her kitchen drawers years ago. You remember those drawers so well; they were filled with recipe cards smudged with thumbprints of grease and chocolate, crumblings of nuts, refined sugars. Beneath the cards there were photographs turned upside down. You could see that there were dates, names, places written on them.

You wanted to know who were these upside-down people. You were fishing through the photographs. There were pictures of you and your cousin holding hands in the back yard in your Sunday best. There were pictures of you bracing yourself against the stone oven. Then there were pictures of Alphonse, a sullen face looking out towards the sky. There were pictures of men in suits with women at their sides. There was one of a woman with a butterfly on her nose. There was another of the woman who used to live next door; she was sitting with your Uncle Léo. At the back of the photograph there was an inscription; it read some-

142

thing like: *Avec Amour, Céleste*. You recognized the *mambo*'s name, the woman Uncle Léo warned you to stay away from because she knew the secrets of *voudou*, the secrets of the ancestors. You are young and don't fear unknown things. When you heard Grandmother's sure steps making their way towards you, you slipped the picture into the back pocket of your jeans and turned to smile at her. You asked her to tell you the stories of the pictures, if she could remember. Your grandmother sighed but you insisted and then she told you all of the stories – except for the one you were holding captive in your pocket.

Later that day, you sought out Alphonse and asked him to speak about his mother and his unknown father. He would not speak to you. You taunted him. Your father is a gi-go-lo, you say. You could not stop yourself. You made him fetch water for you. And just as you were about to show him the picture as proof of his father's evil ways, he threw the water on you. The water was cold and clammy; it soaked through your shirt and revealed the outline of your breasts. This exposure made you angry. You kept the photograph to yourself. You decided to give the photograph to his mother who will be devastated to know that the *mambo* was once one with the man who fathered her only child. You had it sent to her without a word, by a child wandering aimlessly in the street. You gave that child a worthless coin for her trouble and that was that. Will you remember the moment when Alphonse came to you, body trembling, tongue thick with terror, to tell you of his mother's shrivelling to nothing, her mind a web made of fear. The house could do with some airing out, you told him. You had no sympathy for his loss.

Jo, how do I bridge the distance between us?

What moves you are images, images like colourful polaroids that capture fleeting and meaningless moments: a woman in tattered clothing emerging from a cardboard box wedged beneath an advertising placard for Evian water, a naked child of no more than two trailing after her; a boy with a leg which has rotted off at the knee-joint, hobbling on a cane made of a tree branch; a ghostly figure dressed in white from head to toe walking slowly through the yellowish light of a street lamp; a nude woman rising from the ocean onto a coastal road fallen into disrepair, a blue

143

dress folded neatly in her right hand; children with distended bellies and red kinky hair; orange dogs eating spilled rice in the middle of a crossroads. These images move you because the lives you glimpse in them are so far removed from your own. You feel pity, but it doesn't affect your perception that this is how things are – regrettable but in the nature of things – the survival of the fittest. Occasionally, you put your distance aside, make a grand gesture, touch someone, feed a belly, respond to the despair. You think you respond because it is a choice marking your privilege, preserving you from falling into mind-numbing hopelessness. You can as easily do something as do nothing. You will not admit to yourself that these things matter.

When will I hear your voice again?

There will be a time when you look back and you will wonder who invented love, this act of pairing yourself off with someone who is just as lost as you are. You will remember not wanting love. You will remember searching for other souls filled with anger. You will empty yourself of your loneliness against the bodies of young boys who, like yourself, have nothing to lose. You will remember the boy, Eric, who became a Macoute a few days after you had known his body, a mathematical equation of strengths and weaknesses. You will remember his brutality, the lack of kisses, the bruises left on your upper arms, your thighs. You will remember laughing at him to keep your bewilderment from being revealed as he withdrew and pulled himself away. He was the first and he will not be the last. There will be others but none so brutal.

Josèphe, I write you my letters. They go unanswered.

There is still your grandmother. You remember her heaping platefuls of food, the days spent in her yard playing with your cousins, parties. You remember the look of things, the bright yellow of the door frame, the pale blue of the walls, the votive candle lighting the statue of the Madonna. There were days when you lay there thinking only of the day you could depart, fly away to a new land which was of the here and now, not of the ancestors. And yet, you believed in the happiness of those times, so long ago. You came to like the way your grandmother could kill a chicken best of all. That was when you realized that love and hate could

144

go hand in hand, like kindness and cruelty. You were not related in blood, but she was really your grandmother in your affections. You knew this and it made everything you saw and felt seem like a dream, so faraway, and you did not even feel it worth the effort to explore your feelings; it was just a flicker of emotions across your synapses, perhaps to be remembered later. It did not mean much to you at all.

And there is Grandmother, lying on her death bed. Your grandmother. What would she feel of your thinking that blood was just physical matter? Would that thought make her rise, cure her illness, bring energy flowing back into the veins of her tired body?

There was the day she looked at you with eyes now hidden behind dark and ashen eyelids, so full of compassion, and asked what could be the matter with you, throwing yourself away as if tomorrow could not matter. You told her to leave you alone, averting your eyes so as to reveal nothing of yourself. How much you wanted to be held that moment, to unburden your soul, to be mothered. It is easier for you to reject than to risk love; it is just as easy as feeding a child in the street and then walking away because that child is not your own; not your flesh and blood. And that was what you thought when Grandmother put her hand on your thin shoulders and asked you again what she could do for you. All you could do was shrug and look away from her tender and open face, a face that revealed its wounds and seemed not to mind having those wounds opened and reopened, as if life was meant to be a cutlass chipping away at you like a stalk of sugar cane in the plantation yard.

Your grandmother's face is still before you. It pains you. You drag your heavy bones up from the chair, your flesh sinks downwards. This must be how the old feel. You do not know. Perhaps you will never grow old. Perhaps death is in the living.

You turn and find yourself face to face with your grandmother. She is standing before you, her rounded body blocking the doorway. She is wearing the apron she used to wear when we were children. Her hair is pulled back in a bun. She is holding a mirror in one hand and a flower in the other: childhood things. She is nodding her head at you and there is a smile playing on the edges of her lips. If death has a smell, it is then that you realize that it has a scent like wilting flowers in a vase – an acrid, swampy smell. The body is made of water, you think; like a plant, it needs tending. You are thinking of your own body, your back scraping against the most unlikely places – changing room walls, tree trunks, weeds – another body pressing into yours. Then you realize that it is your own body, not hers, evaporating into the air.

You are so very tired but Grandmother is nodding at you saying yes, look, you are so very young, time is on your side. But time is like an echo. It is a fiction. It is a reflection. It does not stop for you; it evades; it climbs back into you like a serpent when you least expect it. It steals you from yourself through your memories, twisting your sense of self into a contradiction.

You turn back to drop your bones into the chair. Grandmother is still lying there, breathing with difficulty, eyes closed, face still. Perhaps there is something to this exhaustion. It may be that it is not life at all which has brought you to this point but your fear of living itself.

Will you never return to us? Has Haiti chérie lost you too?

CHAPTER TWO

Nèg rich cé mulât. Mulât pòv cé nèg.

Can you imagine these being the last words spoken to you as you tell the man who has promised to love and cherish you for all eternity that you cannot go on in your life, that you need to change, become better than you are, and that you want him to follow you in this new way of seeing the world? *There is only this way*, he is telling you, as he laughs in your face and pulls out the braid that confines your long, curly hair. *There is only the way of the one who has and the one who has not.* He laughs and falls back against the pillows, and you watch his chest, the red-brown colour of rust, fall and rise spasmodically. You don't remember ever having been this funny before. Usually, when you try to make jokes, he never laughs but ridicules you or talks over you about some business which is more important than whatever you have got to tell him. You watch his chest rise and fall and wonder what you are doing naked in bed with this man who has promised to make your life worth living. All you want now is to be put out of your misery, never to hear this laughter again. And when it continues, you realize that what you have told him has come much too late, or that you should have kept your thoughts to yourself.

When he finally stops laughing, you hardly notice because you are caught up in the web of your thoughts. You are thinking: how will I ever get out of this? How did I get here? Why did you love this man? He says to you: *Look at your skin – is it not the colour of ripe plums, is it not pale like coffee cream? Why would you throw such a gift away? If you leave here* (and now you notice that his eyes are telling you that "here" has nothing to do with your home, but with the span of his arms, the tightness of his thighs around your body, the rectangle of the bed you are both lying in), you will lose that privilege. *Mulât pòv sé nèg*, he hisses. The venomous way the words spew out of his mouth, makes you understand that you have already shifted positions in his mind. You are no longer the woman of the pale skin whom he loves and will protect until the world knows no rainbows. You are no longer the woman he has planned to keep captive in a fortress he has had your uncle build for him next to the family's summer home in Kenscoff. No, you are not even a woman. You are something he has owned that he no longer has use for. You feel this as the rumpled sheets covering your body are pulled back by hands you now realise have held guns and pulled triggers to push bullets into the flesh of those he saw as he now sees you: something to use and throw away. And you let him use you this way one last time because there is no use screaming, no use protesting, no use trying to make him love you again. This is as good as it will ever get.

Your mind cannot think through another word, another motion. There is only the hope of fleeing one day. You will do it when he is not looking at you with those serpent's eyes, when he no longer sees you at all and someone else with flesh the colour of peaches has taken your place in the bed. That day, you will flee with the only things that mean anything to you: a dress your grandmother gave you that you never used to like because it reminded you of market women, a photograph of yourself and your cousins, fruits that grew in the trees of your Tonton's back yard that you never took the time to dust and eat. You say your goodbyes to the only person you truly cared for, but were afraid to love, Alphonse, and you leave behind the house which is the only home you have truly known. It is Charles' home now. Charles is the son you never were: Uncle Léo's boy.

And yet, it is in the underground movement that love came to find you. You realize that your life is a mystery as it is unfolded to you by your new and undeserved love. She begins by whispering into your right ear: *Je te voulais. Je t'en voulais.* You look into her face and are afraid of what you will find there, in the pale brown orbs the colour of a peach nut. *Je te voulais:* I wanted you. *Je t'en voulais:*

I despised you. She explains: *The others thought you were a fool to have left all those riches behind, back there in the hills, away from the masses, the uncleanliness. I imagined what you were like in that other world: probably plump in places – around the calves, your backside – like someone who had always had a little too much, who could nonchalantly leave mounds of food untouched upon her china plate.* She tosses back her head and her mouth opens into a derisive smile: *I imagined you ate every day on the very best China engraved with miniature French horses trotting in their finery around the gold embossed edges.* She laughs: Nothing but the best for you. And then her face grows sombre as if a cloud has cluttered the blue sky of her thoughts.

Je t'en voulais. You see her searching for the words which will not hurt, the words to part the clouds. She whispers into your left ear: *I envied you. I wondered what courage could have driven you down from the big houses, away from the parties, the late nights drinking rum in a living room the size of a schoolhouse out here. Ah, and what money, what trips! How could you give it all up? And for what reason? When you came to us, the others embraced you quickly. I could not. But then everything changed in how I saw you. Or, perhaps I saw you for the first time. It was the day I watched you when your relatives stopped in the streets uptown to hurl insults your way. Your Tonton screamed the loudest: La voila. La pute. Tu n'es plus que rien. I could see the stiffness of your back as you stood hard and straight against the onslaught of these words. You turned to face him and a soft wind lifted the flaps of your thin cotton dress to reveal your breasts. He fell silent, shamed, and hurried back to his car. I could not tell if he was quieted by your nakedness or by the guilt he must have felt knowing he was, in some way, responsible for the state in which you now found yourself. Your breasts were flattened, shrunken from hunger. That day, I saw how much you had changed since you became one of us and of how much I had refused to want to know you. Suddenly, I wanted to be that cool cloth against your skin, opening and closing, exposing and enclosing.*

Je te voulais. The words stumble from her lips like pearls as she kisses you, her tongue seeking your warm and hungry mouth. Her tongue is like an Anjou pear: ruddy-red, slippery and sandy-soft, travelling over the map of your skin. She returns to comfort you with a smile and rests her head on your chest: *We all talked of who would love you first. I did not believe it could be me. After all, you were a rich girl. One of them.* **Pas des nôtres.** *Not of us. There was nothing I could want from you. Or so I thought – for a time. You resisted and yet you were prized. You held yourself so distant and I began to see we were the same, so alike.* You listen to her breathing, feel her breath spreading itself over you like an unexpected breeze on a hot, dizzying afternoon. Your head is spinning as you try to make sense of her words: you are like a sea sponge taking in the salt with the sweet.

You look deeply into her face – eyes set apart from each other in perfect proportion, like two smooth stones embedded in sand, kept there by the relentless tide. There is no fear there. You reach for her face and bring her lips to yours. *Je t'en voulais.* She asks you often to tell her of the places you have seen; places she dreams about. You describe everything your eyes have ever taken in so that it may become hers. *Je te voulais.* Her body encases yours. She is every place you have ever visited, every landscape yet to touch. Your bodies sink into each other slowly like water seeping into clay. *M'renmen ou.* I love you. *M'remmen ou, oui.* Yes, I love you too.

"*Je te voulais, je t'en voulais,*" she sighs. "Now, I have you. Now I've got you."

When did colour cease to be so important? But had it? This thought stays with you for days after you leave your Tonton's house that afternoon thick with spring rains. It runs circles in your mind as you lie beside this woman who has taken you in her arms and given you new life; this woman who opens herself up to you like the branches of a walnut tree laden with tight shells ripening with the seasons; this woman who knows the proverb but will never speak it to you because she knows: *colour is everything: money is everything.* You tell her the story of your leaving. You describe Charles to her: the muscles in his back which made ripples when he bent down to speak to someone – the muscles you thought made him strong of heart as well as of mind. You tell her about the dreams you thought you had shared with him: the way you thought he was always able to be a part of two opposing and conflicting worlds, drinking champagne with your uncle at family gatherings and arguing politics, then, a few hours later, drinking *clairin* on a street corner beneath a flickering lamplight and discussing revolution with all the seriousness of a man who did not know the meaning of the word betrayal.

She looks at you with pity in her eyes as you tell the story and now you understand what you never knew before but suspected: it was you who betrayed. You loved a man who carried hatred in his every gesture, whose muscles were used to tear apart the limbs of women and children.

You loved this man blindly and helplessly because you did not dare to think of those he destroyed in your name. You listened to him talk of revolution and all the time you knew it was a fraud. You listened and knew he was false because you watched him at those meetings making deals over drugs and guns and even other women. You blamed them, the people in the underground in which you finally came to find yourself a home, for making him the way he was. Affiba looks at you and pities you because you did not want to admit that Charles had not betrayed you, you had betrayed yourself. But there is hope, she tells you, a shadow of a smile hiding behind her unblinking eyes, there is hope because you will not betray us, no? You will not betray those who love you without question. And you are grateful to have heard those words coming from those wine-red lips. You are grateful to be accepted for who you are. It means you will no longer have to run away. You are happy, deliciously, as if you have eaten a rare delicacy.

You turn to the woman at your side and hold her eyes in your own. *Je ne te trahirai jamais.* Affiba nods and you smile at each other. You wish you could tell someone of this simple love. There is no one left to tell. And would they care? Would they understand that you are lying now with a woman beneath a sheet printed with multicoloured flowers on a mattress stuffed with the dried kernels of rice? Would they understand that you left the riches of Port-au-Prince and Charles for this unknown place which carries no name, is unmarked on maps? Would they understand that you love a woman more completely than you loved a man and that this has nothing to do with anything which makes one a woman and the other a man? They would not understand. For once, you are glad that you have no way to write yet another letter which will go unanswered, no words with which to write it.

151

Your days go by very slowly. Too slowly at first. You don't know what to do with yourself, where to sit, where to stand, when to speak and when to be quiet. For long hours you watch the children playing in the dirt behind the straw huts which have become their home. You begin to fall into a pattern of sleeping at odd hours of the day because you cannot tell any more what day of the week it is, even though you are told periodically that it is a Monday or a Wednesday or even a Sunday. You cannot tell here because there is nothing that is yours to do.

Eventually, you are given tasks to do. You learn how to make the necklaces from the dried seeds of fruits. You learn how to break open a calabash, drain it, let it dry until it loses its green brilliance and turns a dull brown. You learn how to sew together patches of old cloth to make shirts bursting with colour. All this you do so that the seeds you string together, the calabashes you scrape clean, the designs you create out of scraps, can be taken to market by Mami Céleste. She you have come to understand rather than fear, as she is transformed into a market woman between ceremonies, her long skirts tied around her waist, her braided hair hidden beneath a square of bright-coloured cloth. You never see the money your work brings in; it is not your money but theirs – those who took you in and feed you. You don't want to see the money anyway. You know it will hardly be recognizable, grimy with layers of dirt.

Your days begin to take a shape. And yet something is missing, something is wrong, but you cannot quite put your finger on it.

At meal times you look at the food as if it is foreign to you. Food begins to seem irrelevant, unconnected to your body. You look at cornmeal and all you see is a woman in your uncle's kitchen, bending over, stirring a hot pot. You look at *grio* and you think of riding in the blue-green Jeep with Charles to attend yet another party. You look at *clairin* and you think of that fateful meeting in the bar when you thought that your life was going to change when this man turned to you and asked if he could buy you a rum and Coke, just to see your smile. You look at an ear of corn and all you see is the field he was turning over to build you your house. Food. It takes you back to that place you fled and resented and thought you hated. And now you miss it.

You cannot eat another bite. You cannot eat because you feel that if you do, you will throw it all up, not the food, but your life, that unfinished life you could not face. Somewhere, you think, there is an album of photographs in which you used to stand between the people you called your family and, in those photographs, you are slowly fading away.

You see them sometimes, this far away family. They leap out of cars at you in the middle of the streets on the days you feel like taking a walk and Mami Céleste lets you follow her down to the market where you sit beside her on a crowded sidewalk and watch the people go by. Hardly anyone buys anything. Everyone is selling something. They come to you, this long-ago family, and they call you all sorts of names you never before heard attached to your person. *Idiote. Pute. Salope.* It's true that you don't look the same. Affiba has shorn your long hair down to the scalp because you don't take care of yourself the way you should and she has no time to do it for you. Affiba knows there is something wrong with you, but you refuse to talk to her. You are missing everybody. You are missing the life you hated. You miss the long showers you took in the bathroom next to your room with the pictures of blue-grey dolphins glazed in the ceramic squares. You miss Josèphe. You miss Alphonse. You look at the picture Grandmother took of the three of you so long ago. You see Grandmother's house and its comforting laughter. You wish you could go back there.

And the days begin to fall away in a jumble of thoughts that have little to do with where you find yourself. You remember who you were in that other life. Callous. Selfish. Unthinking. You see Alphonse's face dancing like a candle wick before your eyes and you understand something about his life that you never saw before. You had choices he never had. All those times you snubbed him and treated him as if he was stupid – even though you knew he went to school and had taken the same lessons as you in grammar and history and biology – you were narrowing his field of vision and yours. You were saying that he could never become any better– and you were becoming worse than you could have imagined. You were a child and you were already consumed with hatred. You realize that it was this in you that attracted Charles – and you to him.

153

You remember a day when you asked Alphonse to serve you and Charles coffee in Tonton's library: you thought it would be cosy among all the books to talk about the future and the liberation movement you would soon take part in, together. It did not strike you as odd to be speaking about minimum wages and rest days as you rang the silver bell your father had given Tonton Léo (from one of his trips to the Vatican) to rouse Alphonse from his afternoon nap so that he could pour you a second serving of strong, aromatic café Rebo – the best coffee in the world! You told Alphonse to button up his shirt as he rushed to meet your demands, to make the bell stop ringing in his dreams. It is then that you remember the word-games you used to play with Josèphe after your English lessons at the Lycée, where Tonton Léo used to take you so that you would both be ready for the world beyond the island. Jo liked one word in particular. Betray. Defined as: *to be disloyal to, assist the enemy of (betrayed his trust, his country); give person etc. to enemy. . .* Charles had laughed at Alphonse, who had left the room in silent and resentful embarrassment. You had been disloyal to your friend. You had assisted Charles, the enemy, in destroying what little trust there could be left between you and the boy who had grown up alongside you. Only now do you understand that you have betrayed *ta patrie*, your people. Are you now the enemy? Have you fallen into enemy hands?

Who are you?

You are the girl whose mother left you behind because she did not know who she was. You are the girl whose mother thought a man would make her complete, any man, anywhere. You are the girl who thought she could take her mother's place and benefit from everything she had left you. You are the girl who never knew what it was like to have a mother embrace you at the end of a bad dream. You are the girl who has never known what it means to wake up in the morning and know that the faces greeting you at the kitchen table love you.

You dream for nights on end of a little girl in a long white dress with a crown of flowers in her hair like a little halo. The little girl is praying with her eyes open, holding her hands flat against each other with a rosary made of white beads wrapped tightly around her thumbs and across her wrists. There is a man standing to the side of her. He is smiling and taking her picture. The man is tall and has wavy brown hair cut short – as if he is in the military. Then you notice that he is wearing a uniform, but you cannot tell what kind it is. It takes you a while to realize that you are the little girl and that the man is your father come home to see you take your first communion.

When he shows you the polaroid at the dinner afterwards, he puts his arm around your shoulders and asks you what you were praying for. You look into his eyes. They are green and glassy. You do not know what he wants to hear so you shrug your shoulders because this is what your mother taught you to do whenever you are afraid of disappointing someone with the wrong answer. In your mind you think of the prayer you did make when the rosary was draped ceremoniously across your hands: *Please, Sainte Marie, make this man go away.* And your prayer is answered the next day when he disappears and postcards signed "Papa" come for you from the place your grandmother used to call the father country, France.

You cry for days remembering that last night when, at the restaurant, they brought out a cake made of frozen cream cheese and whipped cream that tasted like a piece of cloud, light and sweet. When you asked your father what it was he winked at you and took a bite for himself. He told you it was all for you, so the name could be none other than *tou pou yo.* You remember that dessert as if it was yesterday and you wish he had been telling the truth.

Your mind is flailing like a fish out of water. You cannot look at food without knowing that it should never have entered your mouth. You are a parasite. You have never done anything for anyone.

You left the home, which was not your home, when your grandmother was sick. You did not send her a word of warning. You did not even go out of your way to walk to her house on the edge of town to say goodbye. You did not write her a card and leave it along with the note to Josèphe. You did not think for a moment what it would do to your grandmother to find out that you had left in this way, as if your life was nothing, as if all the efforts she had taken to make you happy meant nothing. Why did

155

you not speak to her before you left – your grandmother who loved to polish silver because she said the metal filled her with wisdom – your grandmother who made you rice and kidney beans because she loved you? Now, you cannot eat any more because every time you put a grain of rice in your mouth you are betraying this woman who would have died for you.

You are in the streets watching feet go by: Nike. Adidas. Puma. Arrows and leaping panthers. You wonder where they come from, these names and fancy logos. Then you see the wheels go by. You look up and there it is, the hearse followed by your Tonton's jeep going by the *marché*. The market women make the sign of the cross and recite a Hail Mary for your grandmother, who is in that fat black car travelling her to her place of rest. Later, you find yourself speaking to her in your dreams, but this is not good enough. Three times you have betrayed. How do you begin again?

One morning, Affiba interrupts you as you are stringing seeds to make the necklaces. She tells you that you are not strong enough to stay among them. She tells you that you must go back. You do not know what to say. You know she is right. You do not know how to tell her that you are afraid. How does one go back to nothing?

Who are you?

It all comes back to you. Sitting at the school desk. Thinking how ridiculous life was and how much fun it would be to go for a ride in the country with Jo and Alphonse. Conjugating verbs on lined paper. Liking the sound of the nib as you write: *Être.* To be. *Je suis.* I am, my mother's daughter fleeing. *Je serai.* I will be – myself returning. *J'étais.* I was once – untrustworthy. *Je deviendrai.* I will become – an ally.

CHAPTER THREE

Long, long ago, begins Mami Céleste's story. She always begins in this way, invoking a loss we all carry into the world at the moments of our uneventful births. Long, long ago, she continues – for here there never was a once-upon-a-time, only a shadow of a memory which refuses to remain a part of our consciousness – when the forests were too thick with vines and slippery undergrowth to be walked through, when the skies were purpled with the breath of the gods before the heavy rains, when the air was laden with whispers of the story of a girl not yet born, every living thing swelled with hope. It was not only those who walked on two legs who could see their lives opening like the petals of fragrant poinsettias. The calabashes pulled down on their branches, their tight green shells glowing as if a ghost had polished their skins. The coconuts fell from the trees of their own will, as if to unburden themselves of the weight of their milk. And the sea overflowed its shores, leaving trails of salt against the walls of huts which had been built deep into the land, along the edges of the forest. It was at this time, Mami Céleste said, that this story began, the story of one who would write the secrets of our lost memory.

You listen to the story full of disbelief. Long, long ago, you too believed in fairytales and where did that lead you? Certainly not anywhere you would have wished to be. You are all gathered around Mami Céleste's voice, a tightly-knit circle of what appear to you to be the lost and the forgotten. You suppose that this is why this place is called an underground; it is as if you are the shadows of those above, those who cast you off like used clothing, those who don't know what to do with what they could not understand. Those above, whether rich or poor, disdainful or despairing, were safely cocooned in the visibility of their existence, the ruts of their day-to-day lives. Here, in the underground, identity, community, though real, were unstable, the products of invisibility, of unacknowledgment. When you look at the faces around you, they are marked by a longing to belong. But it is as if they are resigned to this non-place, to their non-being. And as you listen to the story of a life which should carry you safely to shore, as on the back of a giant sea turtle, as you listen, a hand clasping yours amidst this desolation, you cannot help but feel as if you are of two worlds, yet belonging to neither.

Long, long ago, Mami Céleste says again, the birth of a girl-child was announced years before she would come to be. It was a magical moment when the conch shells rose one by one across the islands, relaying the message. We would know her by a marking on her left temple, an odd-shaped, dark brown birthmark extending downwards, as if her skin had been torn apart and then healed itself in her mother's womb. She would be strong from the moment she took breath, and if we had any doubt of her identity she would begin to speak as soon as her legs could carry the weight of her bones, to tell us something of her long voyage. At first, her words would seem like the babble of any child. Then the elders would recognize that hers was not the tongue of the people, that it was the tongue of the forgotten, the tongue of their African foreparents. In her they would see the magic of a land they only knew in their dreams, only began to feel in their bones when they took part in the ritual dances which brought them closer to the ancestors. They could whirl and they could sing, but they could not know what it was to have seen that other land, so like their own, yet nothing like their own, more free than their land, yet the anchor to the chains which had been wrapped about their wrists and ankles. As the child grew older, she would be showered with attention, given special plates of food before and after the harvests. The young would make of her a confessor; the old would make of her their good-luck charm, rubbing the tiny points of her shoulders as she sauntered by, always aware of who she was and who she would become. Like a small bird she would flutter from person to person, announcing the glory of a memory which had eluded them all. Her mind was filled with the colours, scents, and textures of another land. And as she grew older, she would unfurl these images carefully in words each of the villagers could understand, as if the source was not the tiny cells of soft matter which occupied her skull but, rather, brittle pieces of parchment discovered in some forgotten cave which had to be handled with care.

But after some years of telling her stories, fragrant like poinsettias, a dark cloud seemed to cover the girl-child's face. The villagers did not know what to do. She was no longer lively but lay limp like a doll made of corn husks. The woman who had birthed her would take her out to lie in the sun each morning in the hope that the soft tentacles of its warm rays would revive her spirits. She lay there, on a multicoloured piece of cloth made by the villagers, and her skin, which was already a deep brown, turned red like the skin of a hot chilli pepper. Her flesh seemed to boil under her skin and rise in fleshy lesions filled with watery pus that oozed from the cracks. The woman who had borne her took her away from the sun and into the deep interior of her house where all was cool and quiet. She wrapped the girl-child in bandages made of spiders' webs and the puffed skin dried, cracked and peeled off. No sooner had this happened, the girl's tongue begun to swell and choke her. The woman who had borne her pulled the tongue as far out as it could stretch and poured sour-sop juices down her throat. The tongue became its normal size but the girl-child lost her voice. All she could do was cry and turn her head to and fro to indicate a yes or a no. The villagers did not know what to do. They were at a loss. The girl-child was becoming thinner day by day. Though twelve years of age, she had become so small that they often had to seek her out by the flicker of her eyes in the darkness of the house of the woman who had borne her. The villagers were deeply concerned.

Every night, when the blue sky turned all colours of red and orange, the villagers would gather in their *hounfort* to speak to the gods. They would feed the gods the richest of delicacies, the plumpest of meats; they offered their bodies up for possession; they confessed their sins and repented through the act of dance;

they prayed that the girl-child's voice be returned to them. And still the girl-child did not move from her bed. Still, her voice rattled against the walls of her chest like seeds in an *ason* and did not emerge into the air.

Among the villagers, there was a woman who felt that they were not doing enough. This woman was one of the elders and it occurred to her that perhaps it was not the gods who needed to be appeased but the soul of the girl-child itself. For was not the soul something sacred and unique? This woman, who herself had known something of that place the girl-child had come from, though through no physical means known to human beings, felt she had the solution. The child had been sent to them to bring them closer to that other land. Though they could apprehend the contours of that land through their rituals, by drawing the vèvès and having their bodies speak in tongues, they could not know what it was to inwardly feel the breach that this child, who was not really theirs, had surely lived through. The evidence of this was written on her face, in that mark which looked like a healed wound, although it was smooth as the skin of a mango. The girl-child was homesick, pure and simple. The woman was sure of this.

The woman gathered the villagers together and told them of her suspicion. The elders nodded gravely at her words. They were grief-stricken at the thought of losing the child, but they walked away muttering to themselves that homesickness was something that had been invented for the spoiled. Surely, it could not be the reason the child had fallen ill. The younger villagers listened to the older woman; they nodded and agreed that the explanation of homesickness was plausible, but they too walked away from the woman's side, wondering just what homesickness was. They had known no other land than this island and they lived close to their mothers and fathers, even when they were full grown. They did not know what it was to feel their hearts breaking at the thought of a place or person who was too far away to be hailed, too far away to be touched. The woman was left alone sitting on a flat stone in the clearing, encircled by the majestic trees of the forest. She listened to the trees as she pondered what to do.

Minutes later, the villagers saw the woman running through

the trees and towards the house where the girl-child lay. They wondered what she could be thinking, running as if this day was ending and the sun would not rise again tomorrow. The woman ran so quickly she did not notice when the branches of trees scratched her bare skin. If she could have taken the time to stop, she would have kissed those pliant branches, she would have embraced them tightly, for it was the whispers of the trees which had provided her with a solution. She ran as quickly as she could to deliver their message to the woman who had borne the girl-child and brought her into their midst.

The villagers watched as she disappeared into the girl-child's hut. The night air was very still and the trees had stopped their whispering. Curious, both the elderly and the young began to walk towards the hut, which seemed enveloped in silence. But when they arrived, it was not quiet that they heard but laughter. The villagers looked at each other and wondered who could be laughing at a time such as this when their whole world seemed upside down with gloom. The oldest among them knocked on the door of the hut with a gnarled cane. The woman who had borne the girl-child opened the door and the villagers peered inside. A bright light greeted their sorrowing eyes, a light like none they had ever known. They could not tell where it came from. The light surrounded the woman who had gone running through the woods and the girl-child. The woman's hands were flying through the air and they could hear her voice rising and falling as she told a story. The story was of a crow who had lost his way in a forest on the other side of the ocean. The villagers recognized the story; it was one of the tales the girl-child had told them of that other world they could not remember. It was then that they heard the laughter again; it was coming from the girl-child's throat, rising above them and escaping through the doorway like the scent of risen bread. She was clapping her hands in delight and her skin glowed like a polished pearl. The villagers sat at the door of the hut and listened to the woman's story until darkness came down upon them. After that day, they took turns telling the girl-child the stories she had taught them. And this is how they acquired her memory.

After months of talking story to the little girl, she grew and

161

grew into a strong woman. Wherever she walked, fruits swelled and trees whispered ancient secrets. One day, she walked into the forest and did not return. The villagers looked for her everywhere, in the nooks of caves, in the hollows of trees but she had gone. But they were not unhappy for they knew that she had gone back to where she had come from. Neither she nor they would ever again be far from home, far from the ancestors. They knew that one day she would walk back into their midst, her stories etched in stone. Mami Céleste finished her story and quietly looked at the faces gathered before her. They were young and old, all shades of browns and reds.

You hope that her eyes will not rest on you but they do. They linger, locked with your own, as if to tell you that this story was meant more for you than anyone else. But when her eyes move on, you wonder if you invented that moment, if she even knew who you were.

You walk away from the group with your heart in your mouth, your spirit tumbling within you, your thoughts a jumble. What to make of all these stories, of Ti-Jean, of Anancy, of Legba, each of whom you know they worship. You have not taken part in any of the rituals in the hounfort. You have not yet been initiated. You are an unbeliever. Stories are just stories.

You walk away with bitterness spreading out from your throat and into your mouth, licking the back of your teeth like a tongue of fire. You would like to scream but it would not be wise to do so. It would not be right. Freedom has its cost in the world of the underground. Freedom here is not quite as you would have imagined: it does not proclaim its presence; it is small and still and quiet like a hare watching the hunter it knows is searching for its soft footprints on the fresh and springy moss at the foot of trees. You enter the hut where you have been living and lie down to fall to sleep. You can only toss and turn, look up at the sky peering down at you through the thatch of the huts. You close your eyes against the stars. Your head is spinning.

For the moment, you have forgotten Mami Céleste's story. All you can think of are her eyes, burning into you like the sun. And suddenly, you feel moss sticking to the curve of your soles as you walk barefoot through the forest. All you can think of is this anger

162

filling you, driving your feet past the sturdy trunks of flamboyants whose red canopies are spreading themselves against the sky like the wings of eagles. You do not know where your feet are carrying you and you do not care.

It is when your thoughts finally turn to the others, to Affiba who held your hand during the telling of the story, to the children who sat with their mouths hanging open as if they were being fed sweets, to the clasped hands of the elders who listened to a tale told many times over as if they had never heard it before, it is then that you begin to hear the crackling in the forest. Branches snap, foliage crumbles beneath some unknown weight. Your anger turns to fear. Your bitterness to apprehension. Your stomach knots. You stand still, eyes open, ears open, all attention. Then the bodies stumble before you, laughing at you, fingers pointing at your fear. You have been followed by a small group of children from the encampment. You breathe relief. It was not your armed enemies, men in dark blue or army fatigues. And yet, you hesitate to venture a smile.

You stare at the oldest in the group, a boy named Frantz who must be eighteen or nineteen. Although you are almost ten years older than he is, you fear him. You fear his quiet assurance, the certainty of all he stands for. Since the day you arrived, he has kept out of your way. When your paths threatened to cross, he would look right through you as if you could not exist for him, as if he had better things to take in with his eyes. It surprises you now to look into these eyes to see not hatred, but pity, a softness you could not have imagined.

Still, you do not smile.

Frantz looks you over, shakes his head. "It is time to put you to the test," he hisses.

His words fall indistinctly on your ears as if through a fog. All you know is that you must follow him and the troupe of children. Now you notice that each is holding a cutlass. A boy standing next to Frantz has a coil of rope wrapped around one of his shoulders; he looks very serious.

They surround you and you are walking along with them, through the paths of the forest, onto the cracked cement of roads leading away from the underground and up towards those who can hold their lives in the palm of their hands. You are walking into Port-au-Prince. The streets are wrapped in fog. Only the fragile light of street lamps cuts through the soupy film in front of your eyes.

You are growing tired when your feet are stopped by Frantz's upheld hand. You are standing in a clump of bush in front of a high wall. From behind the wall the distant hum of music and accented French flows from an open window. You do not know whose house this could be. It does not matter. What the group is looking for is beyond those walls, in the vastness of the dark yard beyond the house. You scramble over the wall with the others, trying not to cut yourself on the broken bottles jutting out from the very top. You hear Frantz's voice behind you. "*On y va!*" he says like a commander leading his troops into battle.

The field in which we find ourselves is thick like a jungle with overgrown grass and vines hanging from trees. We are actually walking through marshland. You wonder how a house came to be built here at all. You stumble through, following the others, until you are standing at the edge of a lagoon. You watch as the cutlasses are swung against the heads of swamp cotton-tails which flee wildly into the water. Frantz is growing agitated, his assurance seeming to seep away with every step. "They have to be here somewhere," he says.

"What are we looking for?" you ask.

He stares at you blankly, "Turtles, of course."

Turtles. You stumble near the water. It is ice cold against your warm skin. "Why?" you ask.

"Food."

After another minute or so of looking, the boy with the rope jumps up and down. He gesticulates wildly towards a clump the size of a wild, dense, rose bush. "*Li la!*" he says in a strangled whisper. He looks like an animated scarecrow, with his patched clothes and scrawny frame leaping against the shredded clouds in the sky behind him. "Ah. Ah," Frantz gasps when he reaches the clump. "Now, that's a turtle," he says with triumph. He calls everyone to him, "*Vin ici!*"

The laughter from the house continues. You can smell the harsh scent of rum in the air. But you are all invisible.

You cannot see well at all but you can make out the shape of the turtle. It is not as large as at first you thought. It is a common turtle, the kind people buy as pets and feed lettuce to. You remember pleading with your mother for one of these animals. Now you are about to kill one, for food. You hold back the boy with the rope with a hand on his arm. "Careful," you say, "*Sa mord*."

He struggles against your hand. "*Sa pa fé anyin. Moin vlé tué li. Lagé'm.*" But you do not let him go.

Frantz is very pleased. He takes off the machete he has tied against his left leg. "We can kill it right now," he says.

The turtle senses its ambush, retreats into its shell. You wish you could do the same. Your feet itch.

Frantz smiles at you. "Aren't you glad you came? You will have the final honours." He turns away from you and points to one of the larger boys who knows how to kill pigs with his bare hands. "You, come here and help me turn it on its back."

The two of them grasp the turtle by the edges of its shell and flip it over. The turtle is like a big rock, its head and legs hidden away in the coarse folds of its flesh. Frantz takes the coil of rope and makes a noose in its midsection. He hands the two ends of the rope to the other boy and tells him to stand behind the head. "Now, when I tell you to, slip this around the head and pull tight. Understand?"

The boy nods gravely and pulls his lips into his mouth and holds them tightly. There is no breeze but the rope trembles in the air as he holds it gingerly above the turtle.

Frantz takes one of the torches from another boy and kneels down beside the animal which is strangely soundless. He places his hand in the middle of the shell. It sinks a little under the weight of his hand. "Everyone ready?"

The others nod.

Swiftly, Frantz places the burning torch in the hole where the turtle's tail is hidden and the animal's head shoots out the other end. "Go!" The other boy quickly places the noose around the neck and pulls tight with both hands. The turtle lets out the worst noise you have ever heard, worse even than the cry of children who go to bed hungry at night. The sound seems human, high-pitched, and the head lolls back and forth; the teeth glisten in the moonlight. As you begin to turn away, Frantz hands the torch back to someone in the group and takes hold of your arm, placing the machete in your hand. "It is time for you to become one of us," he says.

Time stands quiet and still between you as he holds you and the turtle, and dares you with mocking eyes to walk away. You have nowhere to go. You shake yourself free of his grip and hold the handle of the machete with both hands so that it does not tremble to reveal your fear. Perspiration lines your upper lip but you leave the droplets there. The boy with the rope is struggling with the twisting head and implores you with his eyes to do it and do it fast. You close your eyes, bring the machete back above your head and let it drop with all the force you have left in your body. The sound of the machete cutting through the turtle's neck is like the snap of a breaking bone. Then, there is the sound of a fountain and when you open your eyes you see that it is blood pouring from the cavity onto the already wetted ground. The blood covers your hands and the front of your dress; it is thick and sticky like jelly. You drop the machete and run from the group. You wish you could run up the stairs of Mlle. Dominique's house as you did so many years ago to get help for Grandmother. You trip at the last step and realize that this is another house, another place and time. The voices inside have fallen hushed. The scent of rum is all around you. The revellers inside the house have spilled out onto the balcony. They watch you, unbelieving. You turn from their faces, recognizing among them your uncle's pointed sideburns. Ice clinks in the revellers empty glasses as it melts in the heat of the night. The balcony comes alive with disdainful chatters. You hear the words *"impossible!"* *"sacrilège!"* and then, "police!" You turn to run, to follow the other who have already gone before you, trailing blood as they go, leaving behind them the decapitated head of the turtle to rot and shrivel in the tall grass. As you run, your clothing stiffens with dirt caking the dried blood. Your skin has turned the colour of blueberries.

You follow the troupe from far behind, trying to avoid walking in the stream flowing from the mutilated carcass. But, of course, you are already swimming in it, like an assassin. At the encampment, everyone has gone. The police reached there before you did. There are bodies littering the clearing, the *hounfort*. Dead bodies, bleeding bodies. There are groans, last minute confessions, gasps for air. You run to find Affiba but cannot find her among the bodies. But in the clearing where you last sat gathered, one body writhes in its private pain. You recognize its shape, the cloth tied around the head, the blue dress wrapped around the thickening, elderly body of a woman. It is Mami Céleste. You go to her, hold her head against your thighs. She looks up into your eyes, a knowing and longing look. It is minutes before you realize that she is gone. You close her eyes for her. You wish you could sleep. You close your eyes.

You open your eyes. You are lying in the hut you share with Affiba. Your eyes see stars couched in the sky like grapes entangled in the vine. It is dark and still all around you. You don't know how long you have been asleep. You hear children playing. You rub your eyes. You rise. You stumble out into the clearing. Mami Céleste is sitting there, telling a story. Frantz is sharpening his machete.

Affiba is bent over the carcass of the turtle which is set on its back as if nothing has happened, as if it might be playing a game of hide-and-seek. Affiba takes the knife in her right hand and keeps the shell from rocking with her left: the knife is like hot metal through butter as it pierces the walls of skin holding the bottom shell to the domed husk. She lifts it up and scrapes off the lumps of flesh until they fall softly into the empty hull like jelly. You cry at the sight of the eggs.

Mami Céleste's shadow falls upon you. You have not heard her coming towards you. She kneels before you, pulling her skirt between her legs to form a hollow receptacle for your hands. She holds your bloody fingers in her own and says, "If you do not know what you are doing, you had better not stay here."

You cry against her shoulder and take in the smell of jasmine and cooking oils you thought lived only in your memory of the summers spent with your grandmother when you were a child.

"You take your home with you, Désirée. All is not lost. But you must learn to stop your crying. You must learn to cry like the trees, in whispers."

167

"I cannot go back," you say into her neck. "I cannot go back."

"The decision is yours. Only yours."

You walk towards Affiba. You spend the next hours cleaning the turtle meat in buckets of cold water while the eggs cook in boiling water in which Affiba has thrown some dried pieces of lemon. You watch Affiba's hands as you work alongside one another. Her hands are small, at least half an inch smaller than yours, but they have the look of hands which could once have held the world in their palms and would do it again if it needed remaking. The veins on the backs of her hands stand out like rivers coursing their way through the pale brown skin. The skin of your hands is shrivelled like dried dates from prolonged contact with the water; the slackness betrays you. You left this work to other women like Affiba all of your life.

Watching her work, you are reminded of the cookbook Grandmother kept in a drawer by her noisy frigidaire. *Cuisinière Contente* had a bright green cover and the silhouette of a Haitian woman with bouncing locks happily carrying a tray of steaming food to some unknown destination. In the opening pages, the writer advises her apostles never to hire a cook with children because she would be too distracted, too difficult to manage, always worrying about distant souls and not the stomachs of those who paid her wages. Affiba was one of those women. You are becoming one of those women. And you are childless. And you have children. And you are difficult to manage.

CHAPTER FOUR

Blue is the colour of truth. So it is said. So it has always been. Truth: *Vérité* cannot be translucent, clear like the water trickling naturally from secret springs buried deep within the mountains of this land. The mountains have seen better days: their trees were felled like matchsticks by the yellow metal cranes sent by the Americans in the early years of this century, leaving the ground red like an open wound exposed to the tortures of the sun. But see how the mountains resist: the patches of green piercing through the surface to touch the air, the waterfalls erupting against jutting clumps of black rock. *Vérité:* Truth. It is like these *mornes*: you cannot see through them and yet they are beautifully vibrant, naked, yet closed to prying eyes. They hide their brilliance like the waves of the sea reflecting the blue of the sky. The colour of truth: so it has always been: so it is said today.

The woman in white robes turns her back to them while her voice is carried away on the wings of the wind to circle above their heads. Echoes of waterfalls rain upon their ears. It has always been this way. Unfathomable.

Désirée watches from the outskirts of the circle, her back against the peeling wood of the outhouse. The acid, rank smell of waste burns her nostrils. She wonders how the air can hold both death and rebirth in its embrace like this. The rebirth takes place before her eyes like the unfolding of a rose or a lily. Every movement occurs smoothly in a preordained order, which is the cycle of life itself. Every movement repeats itself, swallows the other, overlaps, turns over on itself, becomes another, becomes

169

itself. Désirée feels her soul rising out of her, moving outwards from her solar plexus to meet the movements in the circle. Her back is to the outhouse and she is moving towards rebirth, rising like the dusty ash of a defecated self. And it is beautiful: all the things she was taught to despise, ridicule, fear: now she is this unknown she was taught to turn her back on: she is the despised, the ridiculed, the feared. She is finally becoming herself. Désirée watches, listens, and is more silent than any silence she has ever known.

The drumbeats echo in the air. They are slow and thunderous like the hooves of horses falling and rising from the stickiness of heavy mud – mud brown-red like blood which has seeped into the earth. Those hooves suck the blood from the ground. The flat hands of the drummers fall on the stretched mouths of the drums made of hollowed woods, painted with *vèvès* of Damballah and Ezili pointing to the four corners of the earth. The drums announce the group, naming them from largest to smallest.

FAP! The *mama*, so named for the mother of us all, Ezili robed with the truth of humankind's double nature – purity and greed – and the earth through which the current of the beat is channelled all the way to the ground which lies hidden beneath the darkling sky. SAP! The *seconde*, so named for the one who follows the mother, holding up the earth like a coiled snake ready to obey her wishes, divine, supple energy of the cosmic underworld. AY! The *kata*, so named for us children who are seeds upon the earth, spreading ourselves far and wide, wrapping ourselves in the cloaks of our foreparents' stories, echoing their words. FAP! SAP! AY! The drummers' hands strike the drums with the curved horns of goats whittled into the shape of the crescent moon. Their open palms caress the bodies of the drums, forcing the sounds to stay longer in their bellies, hidden from sight, waiting to rise. FAP! SAP! AY! The devotees have arrived. They walk out into the clearing from four corners, dissecting the circle as if it were a pie. They are walking from the four cardinal points of the earth, that which makes us what we are: earth, air, fire and water. All held together by one force: Ezili in a darker hue: Mawu-Lisa, goddess of Africa.

Désirée hears the faraway continent calling to her from the

other side of the island. She expects the supple bodies of Ashanti warriors to come spilling over the mountain ranges, ready to celebrate a liberation which has yet to reach its completion. And here they are, faces glistening, painted in white and black, carrying canes carved with strange human shapes which flow from the softness of the pale pine, cloths of blue and red tied with cords of twine around their narrow waists, devotees who are the gods of the earth.

These figures spilling from the mountainside approach the priestess like clouds crossing a clear sky. As they descend into the circle, they beat their canes in unison upon the ground, as if they are scattering thunderbolts far and wide. Each blow of wood upon the earth is punctuated by an imperceptible movement rolling from one figure to the next, like waves lolling into each other with the rise of the tide as night falls and the water froths and grows in power against the strip of sand trying to stand its ground. The rolling shape of these figures works against the wind in just this way, finding a space where none seemed possible. The wind is harnessed into the harmony of movement, like the froth softly carving away at the sand, softly carving away at the doubts of unbelievers – if there are any in their midst.

In the rolling *danse zépaules* the waves break apart to reveal the rounded shoulders of the devotees falling and rising to the rhythm of the drums: FAP! Shoulders lift in unison into the air. The wind whips above their heads. SAP! A roll backwards into the air. Lungs expand. Arms spread wide like the span of eagles' wings. AY! A fall forward. The muscles of the back contract and stretch as the hundreds of canes are thrust forward. FAP! SAP! AY! Again. Up. Back. Forward. FAP! SAP! AY! With each movement they are purifying the air of the clearing, freeing it of any evil spirits which could wish them harm. They cleanse the earth of its blood-letting, the air of its putrid smells of decay. They replace it with the salty scent of the sea, the sweet scent of home.

Home is a faraway notion for Désirée. She watches the dance with eyes as vibrantly alive as the leaping of the burning *flambeaux*. Overwhelmed by what she has never before had the privilege of seeing, she trembles against the boards of the outhouse. The rough planks bite into the flesh of her thin shoulders. She is suddenly hungry for the fruits she piled into the paper bag on the day she left Tonton Léo's house, hungry for the green passion fruits she watched Alphonse pluck for her at the break of dawn, hungry for the *quenêpes* whose bitter skin she made sure not to touch with her tongue as she bit into them to extract the pale orange nuggets, sweet and soft as a lover's tongue. She thinks of Charles, once the love of her life, and how he has betrayed her with his deceiving talk of revolution. It occurs to her that he is much like Jo's grandfather, Gustave the Martiniquan who, it was said, spoke constantly of freedom for the masses while he led a life of opulence, even of decadence, though he eventually died for the words he printed in the newspaper which had made his fortune. Gustave and Charles. How did they do it? How could they make promises with one hand and reap the benefits of the despairing with the other? How could she, Désirée, have been so blind after hearing all the stories about the grandfather who had left his second family with little other than a roof over their heads? She had wanted to believe that words could carry the weight of the world, the light of hope, love in all its brilliant shades: ethereal, changeable but always strong like a rock.

Words. There are no words circling her now, no words falling like feathers on her head. She had thought that words made her world – that cocoon of warmth which felt like home – safe, secure. But not one word travels through the air from the lips of the devotees before her. As her shoulders rise and fall with each beat of the canes and drums, Désirée feels her old sense of self fall away. She is ready for an existence not blinded by empty knowledge or the smugness of privilege. Hadn't she given it all up? Hadn't she readied herself for something entirely new?

Désirée does not know what awaits her but she does not close her eyes against the startling scene before her. The bodies swelter beneath the hot sun. Each head is covered in a differently coloured cloth: a swirling patchwork of silk. She moves away from the blanched boards of the outhouse, away from her former self. A smile flickers on her face. Her lips part, lips which are lined and creased like dry autumn leaves parched by the wind.

Earlier that morning, before the concert of crying roosters

flowed from street to street and the sun rose like a ball of fire above the hills, Frantz, the leader of the youth, left the settlement behind and hurried towards the brick church on the outskirts of Pétion-Ville where many of their grandparents had been buried. He made the sign of the cross as he passed the wrought-iron gate to the cemetery and waved to the gatekeeper who tipped his military hat cordially towards his lithe figure. Frantz was grateful; the gatekeeper was giving him right of way. Military garb was not always something to be afraid of, though he wondered whether there would ever be a time when fatigues would not be regarded as a sign of status, power. Frantz remembered how he himself had wanted to carry a gun, have a long blade hidden in his calf-high leather lace-up boots, wear gold-plated aviator glasses. He had wanted to be Mr. GI-Joe. Mr. American. He laughed bitterly. Now he wished he had the power to rip the country to shreds, bit by bit, and built it up again into what it should have been after the wondrous Revolution he had read about in books.

He was now a few steps away from the heavy portal of the church, which was locked against intruders. He was a son of God. He did not shrink at the sight of the heavy, rusted padlock. The Lord would show him the way in.

It only took a minute to climb through the window at the back of the church. The priest had not yet come to prepare for the morning masses but there was a font still full of holy water by the wooden doors of the confessional box. He pulled out the flask hidden beneath his shirt and dipped it below the surface of the water. When the flask was full, he lifted it out quickly and closed it with an aluminium screw top. He made the sign of the cross on his forehead with the droplets of water that fell from the lid, then climbed back out of the sacred space through the opening the Lord had seen fit to reveal.

As he waved to the gatekeeper on his way back out, he felt the weight of the flask jiggling against his chest. There would be holy water to sanctify the proceedings later that day.

The water is first used to make the sign of the cross on their foreheads, to keep them in touch with the eternal that lives within each of them. Now, what remains of it has been poured into a hollowed-out gourd. The *mambo* holds it above her head and closes her eyes to murmur words of thanks to *Bondye* up on high. The celebrants need her blessing to support them through the ritual baptisms which are about to take place. These baptisms will rip through their souls and shake them to the core: only the strongest will survive. The rest will disappear back into the underbrush, to emerge again only when there are times of upset, or enemies who threaten them to their last breath. The *mambo* sighs as she finishes her litany and brings the rough brown container to her lips.

Frantz looks on as the water disappears into the *mambo*'s mouth. He wonders what holy water tastes like, if it is clear-tasting like bottled water, or heavy with sulphuric matter like the water from the Stinking Springs, where a dip can cure the most raging infections. Maybe it is thick with the weight of its purity. Only the priestess could know.

The *mambo* is not taking the water into her mouth to taste or drink. Never once does she think about the qualities of the water itself, but of how she will make use of the vessel of her mouth to bring the goodwill of *Bondye* to his followers. The *mambo*'s eyes close and her face turns all the way back to the sky. She holds her arms wide apart; pushes her chest out towards the middle of the circle. All the muscles in her neck bulge as the water comes pouring from her mouth in a perfect arc, bubbling streams of translucent crystal which cascade down into the centre of the *vèvè*. This drawing, made earlier that morning, to greet the devotees with a reflection of their own prayers, has two lines meeting each other at the centre of a checkered heart, which then pull in four directions each of which ends in the swirling shape of an arrow-head. When the last drop of water trickles from her mouth she waits for a piece of white cloth to be handed to her by the nearest devotee. She brings this cloth to her mouth and sponges out the remaining traces of the water. It was said that if holy water remains in a mortal mouth it will eventually burn off the flesh until nothing remains.

Désirée's eyes are burning. If only the pain would stop. If only she could stop resisting the scene before her. They say it is often this way for those who have never seen truth in all its terrifying brilliance. First there is the desire to partake, then the impulse to pull back, look away, pretend that new knowledge has not been acquired.

Désirée closes her eyes against the sight of the waterfall coming from the mambo's mouth. It reminds her of doing the washing two days ago, when the sun was hot and all she could think about was how white the sheets would become as they blanched in the heat. It reminds her of work and toil, not of beauty, not of the springs coming out of the mountains where she was sometimes taken to bathe naked amongst the black rocks, all the children laughing as the waters tumbled over their angular bodies.

The woman who brought her has told her she might react this way. The woman with deep brown skin and long Arawak hair looked deep into Désirée's eyes, and Désirée had seen something like pity and love: *There are things here your spirit will understand better than your eyes.* Then she put her hand flat against Désirée's chest and let it rest there until their skins formed a bridge of warmth, bodies talking, breathing together: *Let your heart do the seeing. Or else, or else, you may lose yourself in a way you could not imagine before you came to us. You will lose everything.*

Désirée remembers those words and opens her eyes. The devotees have put their canes down on the ground. Their bent backs make a repeating pattern of round, white hills atop the red, red soil. Someone takes her hand and she lets herself be led towards the circle. Her eyes are burning a little less, but her heart is thumping very quickly.

She stands at the edge of the circle. The timbre of the drums has risen in volume like the crash of waves beneath a full and heavy moon. But it is still daylight and from where she is standing she can see the pool of water lying squarely in the middle of the *vèvè*. She turns to the person who has brought her here. The eyes are those of the woman who sat beneath the flamboyant with rain falling on her hair, streaming down her face. But she does not seem like a woman, or like a man.

One by one, following a precise sequence of actions, ten devotees approach the *houngan* holding chickens white as snow in their hands. The necks of the chickens have been rung to kill them without the shedding of blood. The chickens' eyes are glazed and clouded with the emptiness of death. But, for once, no blood has been added to the earth. Later, they will be roasted in pits and eaten at the meal which makes of the devotees a community. Then, the chicken bones will be buried in the fields where their rice is cultivated. In this way, they sanctify the earth and return it to its state of purity.

The chickens are laid in a circle around the vèvè and the drums stop. For a minute, there is silence and all look heavenwards as they sing to Damballah, god of all, of earth and air, of woman, and of man. Damballah, the genderless god, stretching all goodness to the four corners of humanity.

FAP! SAP! AY! One by one the drums begin their revel again. One by one the devotees walk towards the priestess in her blue-white robes and kneel before her. She stands inside the circle of white feathers and they kneel on the other side of the line made by the small inert bodies and they wait for the sacrament. One by one she sanctifies their faith by drawing the serpent sign upon their foreheads with a paste made of the water, the cornmeal, the red earth. One by one they stand and thank her and return to the circle. They pick up their canes and wait until everyone has gone forward. When the sacrament is complete they beat their canes again and the last ritual begins: the dance of atonement. Soon they will see if they have been forgiven, if the gods have been watching their efforts to please each and everyone of them high up in the sky.

Désirée feels the mixture of earth, grains and water harden against the taut skin of her forehead. Her hand is clasping the other's hand beside her and she is following in the dance. Her bare feet are slapping on the soil and throwing up dust. Her ears are following her heart, like the drums thumping noisily in her chest. She opens her eyes and all she sees is white. She cannot tell if this whiteness is that of the robes of the devotees swirling around her, or if it is in her mind and she is about to faint away. She's had this feeling before, accompanied with nausea, when she has been ill with a cold or a flu. But now she is filled only with a rare euphoria, such as she has felt when falling in love, or hoping for love. It is happiness that is filling her. It is attached to nothing else but this mask before her eyes, which is turning blue as she looks up at the sky. This is how the sea must feel, she thinks.

One cannot describe the sound of the drums beating long into the dark. It is too perfect. It echoes the sound of conch shells in some long ago time when the drums had been confiscated and burned in heaps before the eyes of the devotees' foreparents. Now that sound is still here, in this imperfect valley which will wake the next morning to the same long day, to the same worries of how to put food into the mouths of the children, clothes upon their backs, this imperfect valley which is filled with agony and despair and somehow still with the balm of goodness, and hope. The sound is like the wave of a memory, bittersweet and incomplete, treasured because it charts the way of becoming – where one has been and where one has yet to go. One cannot describe the sound itself but the devotees repeat it, make it over and over again until it becomes something other than itself, a dancer in the dance of their consecration.

They lose themselves to the dancer among them, the greatest dancer of them all. They lose themselves to each other as their spirits fuse to the gods above. Angular adult bodies become smooth, convex, concave, fitting into each another. They dance together as one huge wave which will crash upon the shore of the inhumanity they must all face separately, once the possession is over, once they each pick themselves up to walk back into the mountains and their separate, isolated existences. Now, though, they don't think of the morning, or of the growing darkness all around them.

There is no sound so cacophonous as this, so noiseless as this, the dancers tell each other, as the figures embrace, drinking in the waters of the other into oneself. But there is no self left to soak it all in, there is nothing but the sound of yesterday, echoing through each body like a tremor, like palm leaves shed in a thunderstorm.

Désirée follows in the dance. She feels arms embrace her tightly. She feels the beating heart of the other against her own and understands now that she has met herself. The heart of the other is her own. She feels the tongue of the other against hers and meets it as her own. She feels the sweat of the other falling against her cheek and feels rain.

When the drums end their lament to the mountains, the dance

stops. For a moment there is complete and endless silence. Then the figures rise from the red, red earth and salute *Bondye* one last time. They shed their masks, their robes, the coiled serpents drawn upon their foreheads.

The women find the women and walk away to prepare the sweet white potatoes for the evening meal and pluck the chickens clean of their feathers. The men find the men and walk away to dig the roasting pits. As they move apart, each group smiles at the other across the wide clearing, as if waking from dreaming, dreams where water is the sign of peace and blue is the colour of truth. A rainbow glimmers in the distance. The gods are satisfied.

JOSÈPHE
1970-?

"I believe that I shall see the goodness of the Lord
in the land of the living!"
Psalms 27:13

I listen to the sound of the metal keys biting into the soft, thin paper on which I am typing the final words of Désirée's story. I sit back in my chair, its cold steel surprising my warm skin through my thin cotton shirt. I sigh. Nothing is quite as I wanted to say it, but there it all is, sheets of paper thrown to the floor, piece after piece. I pull out the page still stuck against the roller of the typewriter, stare at the black letters still glistening with ink. Should it matter that my memories are borrowed?

"Look here," a voice calls from the kitchen. "I say, look here."

I follow the voice through the dark corridor of my apartment. Gustave is standing against the island, decked out in a dapper, white linen suit. A gold watch chain dangles from his right vest pocket. He strokes his thin moustache. His hair is full of wavy curls and slicked back from his face. His face is smooth, his skin the lightest of browns. He pulls out a pack of cigarettes, "*On peut fumer ici?*"

I shake my head. No smoking.

He looks at me with dismay and puts the cigarettes back in his pocket. He shrugs, "Don't know what you're missing, girl." He crosses his arms. "I've been watching you for hours," he says. "You know what your problem is?" The cigarettes re-emerge. He pulls one out, lights it with a silver lighter. He stares at it, holds it at arm's length for me to see. "They don't make these like they used to. Ah? What was I saying?"

I stare at the smoke of his cigarette. It smells likes nothing. Ash falls from the smouldering tip of the cigarette.

"Ah, yes. Your problem. Your problem is this: You don't know how to let go of things. As a journalist, I can tell you this. All that's worth holding onto in the world are facts. Facts and more facts. The rest is to be thrown away, worthless. That's what I think of your stories. And, anyway, I never left your grandmother on her own to fend for herself. I supported our children. I was there when I could be."

He glances at the kitchen. "Nice place you have here. It's not home, certainly. But it's not bad." He waves his cigarette at me. "So you see what I'm trying to say. You should stick to the facts. Facts are the only things that can save you in this world. You are too sentimental, too..." He waves the cigarette about – it is now a small stub – "too much like your grandmother." Gustave puts the cigarette out in a saucer I'd left on the counter. "It could have been different, I suppose. I could have stuck to the facts: I was married, I had children, I had a good job. But something was missing. I could not explain it to myself until the day I saw Carmel standing there by herself in the market. It was her that I'd been waiting for. Yes. Yes. I know exactly what you're thinking."

He wags a finger at me, "You are thinking: what a coward he was not to leave his wife. Well, in those days, that was the way it was. I was a man and I had money. I could do whatever I liked and not be held too accountable. Carmel, well, she was young, innocent; she trusted me. But it wasn't so much like you said: it wasn't sad and lonely. We were full of life, so happy. Well, I *was* away much of the time. But here are more facts for you: what does a man do when he is faced day in and day out with the corrupt? What would you have done? I had all those mouths to feed. I could not abandon my wife or my love. I did the best I could. I played their games. But who lost in the end? *Tu y as pensé? C'était moi.* Just me: I paid. With my life. Death is a hard thing to face when you have no control over it, no choice in the matter."

He looks at me with sad eyes, "The cell was dark, blood everywhere, slime oozing down the walls, no light. The stink of urine, vomit, defecation. We could hear the cries of those being tortured in the cavern below us. Their cries made the earth floor beneath our buttocks tremble. We held our hearts in our mouths and hoped to die quietly rather than at the hands of some metal jaw, or the sharp leather tongue of a whip. Why didn't you write about that in your story? These are facts, I tell you. Well, you did not know me."

Gustave looks puzzled; a frown crowds his forehead into pleats of skin, "Did Carmel not speak of me to you? She was all I could think of in the final hours. I thought of nothing else." He stops speaking, nods to himself. His head falls forward and comes to rest upon his chest.

A minute or two passes. I notice a silver wedding ring on one of his fingers. He looks up, catches my eye. "It was a gift from Carmel," he says softly. "Well, all this is in the past, all long ago." He passes a hand over his slick hair. "No coffee?" he asks.

"Coffee?" Another man's voice startles us both. The man is outside the kitchen window, looking in. He walks through the window. His clothes are covered with dust. He brushes himself off. "Sorry," he says sheepishly. "I was just looking around the back yard. Cold out there." He looks at me quizzically, "How can you stand it?"

I shrug.

"Delphi," Gustave says, "what brings you?"

"Oh," Delphi says, "I come and go." He smiles at me, "Don't listen to what he says about facts. There is no such thing as a fact. I mean – and I think, Grandfather, that you will agree with me – facts are like memories. You can't hold them in your hands like a newborn, you can't prove anything really existed at any point in time. By the way, I never held Alphonse in my arms."

Delphi turns away from us both and peers at the contents of my cupboards. "There it is," he says triumphantly. He reaches to the back of a shelf and pulls out a grey and blue bag. "The coffee!"

He measures out water and pours it into the coffeemaker standing on the island, fills the filter with the dark coffee grounds, presses the red "on" button. "See, Grandfather," he says, "Stay long enough and you'll learn a thing or two."

Gustave strokes his moustache.

Delphi turns to me and smiles again. "Nothing like some good Haitian coffee."

I smile back.

The coffee drips noisily behind him. "It's good to be allowed in a kitchen again," he says. He rubs the tips of his ears. "I don't know if Alphonse meant to do what he did. I forgave him. It did not take long. I don't know what went on his head." He shrugs,

"Perhaps it was as you thought, perhaps he was so filled with sorrow that he could not see the terror to which he was delivering me. Such terror."

Delphi pats his arms, hugs himself. "The Macoutes got theirs in the end, didn't they? I saw it from above, the *déchoukaj*." He mimes digging up a root, crashing down the gate of a house, stomping on a body. His hands cut through the air like the sharpened blade of a machete. He drops his arms to his sides. "You didn't think I had it in me, did you? But how long can you play the hero? The martyr? I'm not as good, or as brave, as you made me out to be."

Gustave takes out two more cigarettes and hands one to Delphi.

"Thank you, Grandfather," Delphi says. He begins to take a drag on his cigarette. "You see," he continues, "your heart can only take so much." He gestures with the hand holding the cigarette. "You look at all these little children. I mean, you really look at them, right into their eyes. And what do you think you find there? Old, tired souls. In children!" He shakes his head. "It isn't possible to hold on. To your heart, that is. Your heart begins to break and when you put it back together again, it's a little harder than at first it was. And when you try to bring these children back to the land of the living, each time you think you have brought one back to life, another one slips through your fingers, breaks again, and hardens. And finally, what you are left with is – no, not a shell, not the casing, but the pip, *un noyaux*, a hardness like rock. Your mind fights it. You try to work through it. But when you bear a heart turned to stone, what can you do? So, the eyes, after a while, don't make any difference. They do not touch you quite as much. You see them. You do what you can. And then, then, you leave it all in *Fa*'s hands. You leave it to destiny."

"So," he looks at me, "you had most of it right, except for that. In another life, I could have been Alphonse. I could have been just like those children, eyes empty of any light. I could even have been the man who shot me dead, that Eric. But at least I could look myself in the face in the mornings. And that's something. That is a true, true thing." He puffs on his shrinking cigarette.

He stands with Gustave, smoking. Both are lost in their thoughts of their last days on Haitian soil. I watch them, amazed at the presence of their bodies.

I hear the creak of a rocking chair coming from the study. I walk back slowly through the apartment. I stand in the doorway to the work room and see Grandmother as I knew her when I was a child. Her face is free of wrinkles. Her hair is a jet black and pulled back into a tight coil. Her hands are full and plump; her body round. She fits neatly into the *dodine*. The carpet is no longer there; in its place the wooden boards of her front porch, scratched with marks from the rocker; it creaks beneath her weight. It is a comforting sound to my ears. I smile at her. She smiles back.

"You have kept many things," she says. Her voice is barely a whisper, almost as if she has not spoken. "You have all the cards." My keepsake box is buried in her lap. She lifts the cards she used to send to me from the box, smells them, returns each to its place. "Did you read all the inscriptions?" she asks.

I nod.

"Now," she says, "I know I am far from holy. But my father taught me to read the Bible. He told me the words would protect me. I remember those words and, somehow, they did sustain me. Remember? 'Deliver me from my enemies, O my God, protect me from those who rise up against me, deliver me from those who work evil, and save me from bloodthirsty men.' You see, it is all stored up here," she points to her head, "in my mind. You could have thought those psalms were written with us in mind. Ah, Haïti. I kept you from her, didn't I? I felt I had no choice. I saved you from repeating my life; I saved you from the *Macoutes*. But still you were afraid, weren't you?" She looks across the room at me. Then, she plunges her hands back into the box. "You have everything here. What's this?" She pulls out trinkets: a key, a gold medallion. "Ah. Désirée. That's the other thing you lost, isn't it? You must blame me very much."

I say nothing. Grandmother looks beyond me, beyond the room. "Sometimes, I wonder what I could have done differently. But I have told you all this. You have written it all down just as I said it. There were too many things I did not know. There were too many things I did not want to know. You were too hard on

184

Gustave. I knew he was married. I just refused to look ahead. I refused to see. This you know. I missed you. I missed all of my children. It's a strange thing to grow old alone, far from everyone, far from every living thing you tended in your younger life."

She places the trinkets back in the box, closes the lid. "You have to keep these things safe," she says.

I nod. I smile. I do not know how to keep her, how to prevent her from leaving once more.

"Don't worry," she says. "We are written into each other's hearts until time no longer exists. You are my sacred heart and I am yours. *Très simple.* Alphonse, he will not know this for some time. He is lost, as you once were." She shakes her head. "You try, but children have their own ideas. They think you are pushing them away when you are trying to protect them, give them a better life." Grandmother closes her eyes. "I am tired," she says, "so tired, just thinking about that life."

"Who, here, is more tired than I?" Céleste walks into the room, trailing the skirts of her blue dress behind her. She sits down in front of the typewriter. "So," she says, "you were the one. You were the child in the story I told your cousin and the others. Ezili works in strange ways, doesn't she?" Céleste turns to look at Grandmother, "*Hein*, Carmel? Who would have guessed?" She takes one of the pages in her hands. "True, true, much of this is true. But it does not matter, does it, how true it is? What matters is that you have found all of us again."

Céleste runs her fingers across the typewriter keys. "Very nice," she says, "but remember that this cannot replace your tongue." She shows me her tongue. "You see this? This is what kept me alive through the ages. Imagine if they'd cut it off. Such things were done, long, long ago." She shudders and breathes in deeply, as if she can still smell the burning flesh. "Long, long ago, every imaginable desecration took place. It is hard for you to see this, I know. But I saw it all. It was my tongue which allowed me to tell others what I'd seen each time I came back."

She glances over at me. "You," she says, "you knew me only in the days when it seemed that I had lost my head. I remember you and your cousins quite clearly." She laughs dryly, "Always up to some mischief. But you remembered those times as well. Quite remarkable, really. You were a child and yet you were not a child, storing away all the little details of the life in front of you. There's nothing more I can tell you." She waves the sheet of paper in her hands above her head. "This is what I had to say. Never mind the details. It will take you another life time to sort all that out. But this is a start, isn't it, Carmel?"

The two women smile at each other and soon are lost in their own remembrances. Laughter erupts in the kitchen and the three of us rise to meet Delphi and Gustave. Céleste embraces her son around the waist. Her head rests against his shoulder. He pats her hair. My grandmother kisses Gustave and laughs at his moustache. Gustave holds her head in both his hands and looks into her eyes. They break apart and sit around the island to drink small cups of *café*. When they are gone, they leave the lingering smell of coffee grounds, and the aroma of sea salt in their wake.

In the stillness of the apartment, I pick up the dirty cups, the scentless stubs of cigarettes, clean out the coffee maker. I return to the study, gathering the pieces of papers strewn on the floor into a disorganized pile. I return to the photograph of Alphonse, Désirée and I and wonder what it will take to see them each again. Alphonse, I do not know. He seems so distant now, so indifferent and lost. I have not yet made the step to seeking his forgiveness. I have not yet made peace with forgetting. Désirée, however, is my sister. Just like Grandmother, her name is engraved on my heart and I must find her again, before it is too late. I need to hear her story in her own words, from her own tongue.

★ ★ ★ ★

It is early in the morning. The sky is barely beginning to clear, to turn blue as the sun rises. It is too early for me. I'm used to sleeping in at all hours of the day. I glance out of the car window and can barely make out the shapes of trees and the roofs of the houses lining the street. There is a fine mist in the air left over from the cool night. It is late October and the leaves have turned all shades of red and orange. The daily temperatures are brisk, cool, but not yet near freezing. The winter should not be too harsh this year, I think. Most of the houses are still dark inside, their inhabitants still sleeping. I wish I were still cosily nestled in my bed, ensconced in a dream so beautiful, so real, that I wish it were true: myself lounging, sinking into the sand of a beach on the shores of the Caribbean sea. I close my eyes to seal myself in that image but it goes as quickly as it came. I sigh, open my eyes. The light is blinding. I reach in front of me and fumble with the latch of the glove compartment. I open it and rummage through the bric-à-brac inside. Sunglasses. I pull them out, close the door, push the glasses up the bridge of my nose.

"Better," I say to Georges who is sitting quietly in the driver's seat, taking me to the airport.

"What?" he asks.

I point to my sunglasses. "I couldn't see anything out there. My eyes hurt."

"Oh," he says, glancing at me for a second, then back to the road. "I'm sorry your eyes hurt on top of everything else."

"That's life, I guess. Thank God for sunglasses."

Georges scowls, concentrating on the dim road stretching out before him. "Thank somebody," he says.

I smile as I sink back into the seat. I am still half-asleep and dreading the long flight to Miami from Winnipeg, followed by the briefer flight over the Caribbean sea to Port-au-Prince. With my right hand I flip back the lever to push the seat into a reclining position. I lay my hand on George's thigh and rub it lightly in thanks. I close my eyes again and feel his hand come to rest on top of mine. I know his hands so well, imagine their pinkish contours against the reddish brown of my own, the nails trimmed and filed perfectly into square shapes, stripped clear of any trace of dirt. His hand moves softly across mine and then lifts away. "Don't fall asleep now," he says. "Try to stay awake until you're in the plane."

I nod. I keep my eyes closed but move my seat back to the upright position, as if I am already in the plane and warned by a stewardess of our impending descent. Georges is quiet and self-contained, but he feels alone if he's forced to navigate the car with a sleeping passenger. I squeeze his thigh to reassure him that I won't fall asleep but, really I am only thinking about his hands. I know they are turning a yellowish white as he grips the steering wheel, afraid that he might make a wrong turn and I will miss the only flight out today.

"So," he says, "Who's picking you up?"

"I don't know," I murmur.

"You don't know? How can you not know?"

"Haven't we already had this conversation?" I can feel a muscle in his leg twitch through the fabric of his pants. I move my hand and open my eyes. "A friend of Désirée's. Don't worry." I look at George's hands; they are small and fragile for a man's. As I thought, they are gripping the steering wheel too tightly and turning different shades of yellow and pink. "Someone will be there for me."

He looks at me with soft eyes. "Well, I do worry."

When I am seated in the plane and feel the jolt of the wheels leaving the tarmac, Georges somewhere below me, I finally understand why I have held on so long to that picture of the three of us, young and afraid. It was to find out what we did not know then: the measure of our loss.

ABOUT THE AUTHOR

Myriam J. A. Chancy's work as a writer, scholar and photographer has been shaped by her place of birth and by her country of adoption. Born of Haitian parents in Port-au-Prince, Haiti in 1970, she was raised in the Canadian cities of Quebec City and Winnipeg. She completed her first degree at the University of Manitoba, and her Ph.D. at the University of Iowa in 1994. From 1994-1997, she was Assistant Professor of English at Vanderbilt University.

Her first published book, *Framing Silence: Revolutionary Novels by Haitian Women* (Rutgers UP, 1997) was written as a response to the 1994 US led intervention in Haiti, and her discovery that Haitian women writers had first begun to produce novels in response to the US Occupation of 1915-1934. In 1995 she wrote the first draft of *Tou Pou Yo*, later revised and re-titled as *The Scorpion's Claw*.

In 1997, she moved to Arizona State University. Both *Framing Silence* (Rutgers UP) and *Searching for Safe Spaces: Afro-Caribbean Women Writers in Exile* (Temple UP) were published in that year.

In 1998, she wrote her second novel, *In the Hills of Haiti* (revised since and re-titled *Spirit of Haiti* and published by Mango Press. It was shortlisted for the Best First Book Prize, Caribbean/Canada Region, of the 2004 Commonwealth Prize.

In 2000, she was awarded a Martin Luther King, Jr, César Chàvez, Rosa Parks, Visiting Professorship for a public lecture at the University of Michigan and in 2001, a residential fellowship at the Camargo Foundation in Cassis, France. In 2002, Dr. Chancy held her first exhibition of photographs in a one-woman show at the University of California, Santa Cruz.

On leave from ASU, Dr. Chancy was a Visiting Associate Professor of Women's Studies at Smith College where she served as the Editor of the academic/arts journal, *Meridians: feminism, race, transnationalism* (2002-2004).

Currently, Myriam Chancy is working on a third novel focusing on spiritual mysticism in the Caribbean. Having resigned from her position at ASU, she is pursuing a career in the visual arts and as an independent writer/teacher/consultant.

Cherie Jones, *The Burning Bush Women and Other Stories*
ISBN:1-900715-58-9, pages:180, price: £7.99

Delores is losing parts of herself, her typing speed, her ability to say 'hi'
to work colleagues, until she is no longer Delores at all, but bare-footed
Queen Mapusa, child of Africa, proud mother of modern civilization.
Etheline Elvira Ransom is lying in bed, with a pair of scissors under her
behind, waiting to teach her bullying, errant man a lesson. Odetta is a
54-year-old wife and mother talking her way through the day of her
secret abortion. The Burning Bush women are smoking cigars and
weaving each other's wild blood-red hair into tight plaits, but the plaits
won't hold: somewhere, the hair says, a Bush woman is dying.

In these sometimes strange, funny, tragic and truthful stories,
Cherie Jones weaves paths through the joys and suffering of women's
lives. The writing occupies an in-between space between the magical
and the realistic, exploring the tensions between the African folk
wisdom Nanan passes on from the ancestors to her grand-daughter,
and the colonised dictums that the mother in 'The Bride' offers her
daughter about how a respectable woman lives. ('Remember how
nappy you can look if you let yourself go.')

Mark McWatt, *Suspended Sentences*
ISBN: 1-84523-001-9, pages: 252, price £8.99

A group of sixth formers vandalize an exclusive Georgetown club on
the day of their school leaving, coincidentally also the day of their
country's independence. Several of their parents think a lesson is in
order and the semblance of a trial is organized. The sentences they are
given are suspended provided that they fulfil the task set by their
English teacher, who has interceded on their behalf. Each must write
a short story that says something about the newly independent Guyana.

Years later, Mark McWatt, one of the group, is handed the papers of
his old school friend, Victor Nunes, who has disappeared, feared
drowned, in the Guyanese interior. The papers contain some of the
stories, written before the project collapsed when the group realized the
trial was a hoax. As a tribute to Victor Nunes, McWatt decides to collect
the rest of the stories from his friends.

Suspended Sentences is a tour-de-force of invention. The stories,
entertaining in their own right, whether supposedly written by eighteen year olds or in later adult life, work not only like Chaucerian tales
to reveal their teller, but have an affectionately satirical take on the
nature of Guyanese fiction making. By ranging across Guyanese
ethnicities, gender and time in the purported authorship of these
stories, McWatt creates a richly dialogic work of fiction.

Kevin Baldeosingh, *The Ten Incarnations of Adam Avatar*
ISBN: 1 84523 000 0, pages: 452, price: £10.99

'Tell me if I am mad,' Adam Avatar, a copper-skinned man with startling green eyes, asks Dr. Surendra Sankar, a psychiatrist in Trinidad. Aged forty-nine, there is some urgency in his request, since he fears that, very shortly, when he reaches his fiftieth birthday, he will die at the hands of his nemesis, the Shadowman. Adam believes he is nearly five hundred years old and has gone through nine previous incarnations, including living as a fifteenth century Amerindian, a Spanish conquistador, a Portuguese slaver and a Yoruba slave, a female pirate and a female stickfighter in nineteenth century Trinidad. Not unreasonably, Dr. Sankar reaches for his pad to prescribe drugs used to control delusional states.

As the consultations continue, Dr. Sankar's professional expertise is tested to the full. On the one hand, his patient appears to behave with impeccable rationality, on the other, the accounts Avatar brings of his previous lives suggest buried traumas of the most worrying kind.

And when Avatar's narratives of the experiences of his past selves are revealed to have an authenticity that cannot be explained away, Dr Sankar's perplexity grows.

Kevin Baldeosingh brings a powerful narrative drive to this unfolding mystery, a Joycean variety of historical Englishes to the accounts of Avatar's lives and a vivid and persuasive grasp of each historical period. But the novel also asks uncomfortable questions about the nature of power, the relationship between abuser and abused and the malleability of the person in different social environments.

Set in Haiti, Jamaica, Barbados, Guyana and Trinidad, *The Ten Incarnations of Adam Avatar* is an epic account of the New World experience and a provocative enquiry into the nature of history and what it means to be a Caribbean person.
